A WESTERN ROMANCE NOVELLA

GUNSMOKE & HEARTACHE

BOOK 1

Part One of the Trilogy

LILA DAWSON

TWISTED KEY publishing

2025

First Printing: 2025

ISBN 978-1-63911-182-4

Twisted Key Publishing, LLC
www.twistedkeypublishing.com

Ordering Information:
Special discounts are available on quantity purchases by corporations, associations, educators, and others. For details, contact the publisher at the above listed address.

U.S. trade bookstores and wholesalers: Please contact Twisted Key Publishing, LLC by email twistedkeypublishing@gmail.com.

Contents

Prologue
Tabitha Henry
Eight Years Earlier

I clutched Ms. Yates's journal to my chest as I ran down the hallway toward my father's study, my heart pounding with excitement. The leather binding was worn down from her many years of use, so I had to handle it carefully. Yet, it was filled to the brim with her notes, curriculum, and hard-earned methods for handling difficult students… it was gold turned to paper. I'd never expected to receive something so precious for my thirteenth birthday.

"Father!" I called out, barely pausing to knock before bursting through the door of his study. "Father, I have something to show you!"

He looked up from his desk, which was neatly sorted into heavy stacks of ledgers, contracts, and letters. His expression immediately shifted to irritation, but I was confident this would cheer him up.

"Tabitha, how many times do I have to tell you to knock properly before entering? I am in the middle of working."

"Sorry, Father, but this is really important. I've decided once and for all: I'm going to be a teacher. Ms. Yates said I'd be a natural, and she even gave me her journal with all the methods and—"

"A teacher? Really? You're still on that? I didn't think you were actually serious."

"I am serious. I want to make a difference like Ms. Yates has and help kids grow and learn. Ms. Yates says being a teacher is one of the most important callings a person can—"

Father's laugh interrupted me. It wasn't a fun, joyous laugh; I'd heard it before when he thought someone said something especially ridiculous.

"A teacher," he repeated, shaking his head. "My daughter, born into one of the wealthiest families in the country. My daughter, who would never want for a single thing in her life and already has men lining up for her future hand in marriage… wants to be a schoolteacher?"

"What's wrong with being a schoolteacher?" I asked, more defensively than I intended. My excitement was slowly fading into something else.

"Tabitha, sit down. I will explain this to you."

His voice was cold. Harsh. I knew better than to backtalk him at this point, so I slowly walked over and sat in the chair in front of his desk, still clutching the journal to my chest.

"Teaching is for those who have no other prospects, devoid of ambition."

"I'd like to be able to choose my own life," I said, though my voice was weak and barely a whisper.

"As a daughter of the Henry family, you have responsibilities just as the men of the family do. Obligations. You are a beautiful girl, Tabitha, and you will be a beautiful woman. Your marriage will secure an alliance that could benefit our family for generations, just as much as any business deal I could ever craft behind this desk. Perhaps even more so. I thought your mother and I raised you to understand your place in the world."

"My place?" I snapped.

"Teaching school is beneath you. You don't need to lower yourself to things better handled by your lessers. Now, give me that ridiculous book that's put all these thoughts into your head."

"No," I said, clutching it tighter to my chest. It was a desperate plea. "It was a gift. Ms. Yates spent years working on these notes."

"If she had any wisdom, she'd know better than to encourage your absurd fantasies. Give it to me. Now."

His hand snapped out, grabbing the delicate book. For a moment, I surprised myself by tightening my hold. I struggled to keep it.

"No. Father, please!" I shouted. The commotion drew my mother and my brothers into the room as well. They began shouting at me too, my brothers hurling insults I didn't even hear.

Finally, my father tore the book from my grasp.

"Tabitha, I know this seems harsh, but it's for your own good. You'll understand when you're older, and you'll thank me later."

He stood up and walked out of the room. I followed him, shouting. Begging. My mother grabbed my arm, but I tore free, staying just behind him while looking for any opportunity to snatch the journal away.

"Father, I'm begging you. Please, please!"

I was hysterical now, unable to hold back my tears. We walked all the way down the hallway and into the kitchen. A servant was tending the stove when Father suddenly pushed her aside, tossing the book into the flames.

I screamed, running to try and grab it before it was too late. My mother and the servant woman grabbed me before I could. All I could do was watch as it burned little by little. The lessons I hoped to learn from that book had become a different sort of lesson.

That my father didn't love me. Nor did my mother or my brothers. I was an object to be used for the family's benefit. A prize to be won. A currency to be bartered.

"Just look at you, Tabitha! You've been so brainwashed by that stupid teacher that you don't even understand who you are. Who your family is. I expect this to be a lesson to you, and I expect you to learn from it. I don't like it when I'm forced to be this kind of father to you, but you've pushed me too far and left me no choice."

I fell to my knees and sobbed for a long while. So hard I could hardly breathe, and could hardly see through the tears. When there were no more cries left in my throat, and no more tears left in my eyes, I walked away.

I'd made a decision.

I'd become the sort of woman no man would ever want to marry.

Chapter One

Tom Roland

Mrs. Henry made the best sassafras tea in the state, and I'd fight any man to the death who said otherwise. After a long day of hard work—not that I'd ever willingly partaken in one—it really hit the spot. Whiskey was my drink of choice for most of my life, but Mr. Henry didn't allow such a thing on his ranch. Nor did he allow his workers to partake, insofar as he could prevent it. Most of the men rode into town together on a regular basis to frequent the saloon, but I'd aged out of such indulgences.

No. On this, my thirty-second birthday, I was content to sip on sassafras tea as I waited for one of the new boys, sure not to make it through the week, to fetch another bucket of nails to start putting up the new fence. The old one just wasn't cutting it anymore. One of Mr. Henry's steers leaned on a section the day prior, and it folded like an outlaw being offered freedom in exchange for ratting out his friends.

An analogy, although appropriate, that stung a little as it formed in my mind.

"Here's your nails, Mr. Roland. I fetched the hammer too. You didn't mention it, but I figured you'd need one on account of the nails."

Shoot… There went my hopes of buying more time by sending him after the hammer. It felt like a crime to swig down half a jar of fine sassafras tea, but that's what I did. Better than letting it spoil in the morning sun.

"Good thinking. Oh, and you ought to just call me Tom. I ain't old enough to be no mister anybody."

The young man nodded, still afflicted with the nerves of his first week on the job. He treated the suggestion as a scolding, and his face took on a frown that wouldn't go away.

I picked up the pail of nails and had barely extended my hand to retrieve the hammer when the deep voice of Buster Williams, Mr. Henry's ranch foreman, nearly knocked my hat off. Or maybe that was me flinching from the start. Buster was a Black man, near seven feet tall, with a voice that sounded like it belonged to a man twice that size. You'd never know the man was ever a slave. If anything, you'd expect he was the one holding the whip.

"Go ahead and put down that bucket, Tom. Mr. Henry's got a prestigious job in mind for you today, more befitting a man of your station. You've been here a little over a year now, so we'd like to start treating you with the respect you deserve."

I sighed, placing the pail down on the porch and straightening myself. I folded my arms, lowering my head and bracing myself for whatever nasty work Buster was about to give me. The last time he had that tone, I was stuck shoveling manure that had spent two days building up after a new hand quit without anyone noticing. Unfair to blame me for the misdeeds of another man… although I'd been tasked to watch the boy and show him the ropes. I suppose I might have shouldered a bit of the blame.

"Mr. Williams, I appreciate the offer but I'm feeling generous. I'd like to offer whatever task you have in mind to this young man here. I reckon he deserves it after putting up with me all week. I'm sure he's been struggling to keep up with me and could surely use a break from the hard labor."

Buster smiled a broad, warm smile, clearing the several feet gap up to the porch with a single large step. He placed a hand on my shoulder and laughed. His laugh would've hurt my ears from the other side of the property. Face-to-face, it felt like my teeth were going to rattle out of my gums.

"Nice try, Tom. Mr. Henry's niece is arriving soon and she'll be staying here on the ranch for a while. She'll need someone to take her belongings to her room and show her around the ranch."

I narrowed my eyes, making the mistake I often made of speaking before my brain had a chance to vet the words first.

"I didn't think he and his brother were on speaking terms anymore."

"Marcus Henry doesn't employ us to interpret his family business, Tom. You'd do well to remember that. You know it's a sore spot for the man, so I'd advise you not to bring it up again. Go ahead into town and wait for her at the station. She's due on the ten o'clock train."

Good advice from Buster, as usual. Marcus and his brother Robert weren't exactly enemies, and Marcus certainly wasn't a poor man who'd done little with his life. However, their father's mining company was a point of contention between the two men. For reasons I'd never be brave enough to find out, his younger brother Robert inherited the mines solely, leaving a comparatively smaller inheritance to Marcus. More money than I'd ever see in my lifetime, but compared to a lucrative mining company? Let's just say I could understand the man being a bit bitter.

"Yeah, I was wrong to mention it. Alright. I'll get the wagon ready and meet her."

I had a lot of questions. Some I pretty much already had the answers to, and some I'd have loved to ask if I hadn't wasted all of Buster's goodwill on the first stupid thing that popped into my head. I knew better than to ask what the girl looked like. No doubt, she'd stand out like a sore thumb in this town. Marcus Henry was one of the wealthiest men around these parts… but he was no Robert Henry. Though, I valued my employment enough to never say such a thing aloud.

Most of all, I was curious why the great Robert Henry would send his precious daughter to this little town. I doubted it was because the girl wanted to see her uncle. Before today, I'd only heard mention of the girl once, and that was by Mrs. Henry in passing. I didn't recall the exact words used, but I remembered they weren't kind.

***

I managed to roll into town just before the train arrived. Not late, in my usual fashion. Didn't want to lose my head by offending royalty, after all.

The platform wasn't all that busy today, but I was right about it not being much of a challenge to pick out the princess from the crowd. In fact, I was a little surprised by how much she stood out, and for reasons I hadn't expected.

Here I was expecting a little girl, but this was a grown woman. Young, but grown. She had thick, curly blonde hair. It was clean, but little effort had been put into styling or maintaining it. Her blue eyes caught the sun, giving them an otherworldly brightness. Not a hint of fear to be seen in them. In fact, they had the sharpness of a hawk scanning the world below for prey. This girl was trouble, and I knew a troublesome woman when I saw one. She wasn't dressed like anyone would expect a daughter of Robert Henry to dress, but despite her plain clothing, it was clear there wasn't a single tear or stain to be found. Doubtful she'd ever worked an honest day in her life, or even prepped a meal.

I took a step forward, tipping my hat as I reached for her largest suitcase.

"I handled it all the way here. I don't see why I'd need your help with it now," she scoffed as she stomped around me, her small boots rattling the platform as if the soles were somehow filled with lead.

I took hold of the suitcase again as she passed, yanking it from her grip.

"I was asked to help you with your luggage, miss, and I ain't about to sit here and watch you drag two armloads of it around like a fool while I loiter about and watch."

Those eyes of hers really did give the impression she was looking right through a man, and not really seeing him as a man at all. She might not have been dressed like royalty, but she sure enough acted the part. After a moment, it began to feel awkward. Like I'd been pulled into a staring contest without warning. Clearly, she expected me to give in and hand her luggage back. Just so she could go and tell Mr. Henry I didn't lift a finger to help her? Not a chance.

Eventually, she relented, huffing loudly and rolling her eyes.

"Fine, just don't break it."

Her hand was gripping her other luggage so hard her knuckles were white. Her cheeks were flushed. You'd think I slapped this woman based on her reaction. Typical rich brat. This was sure to be one of the longest wagon rides of my life.

I helped her load all of her luggage in the back. As expected, she refused my offer to assist her in stepping up to her seat, leading to several clumsy attempts before she finally managed it. It took everything I had not to laugh, but I managed in the end just as she did.

As we began to move, she only stared ahead, clenching and relaxing her fists absentmindedly.

"So, what brings you to—"

"Don't feel obligated to make small talk. You were asked to help with my luggage, and you have."

I took a deep breath and sighed.

It would definitely be a long ride back.

Chapter Two
Tabitha Henry

I hadn't been on a train since I was a small child, but I quickly realized my memories of the experience were rose-tinted. Three seats back, a child cried incessantly. To my left, an old man reminisced about the war.

It never ceased to amaze me how many men romanticized such an awful thing. They dreamed of a time when they could return to the battlefield and kill more brothers, fathers, and sons. As if I needed more reasons to hate men and everything they stood for. We'd all be better off without them.

My father, most of all. All the other girls believed that, because my father bought me expensive gifts, it somehow meant he treated our family well. In reality, he treated our home more like a prison. Every action was planned and dictated because he knew better. My brothers were given complete freedom to pursue whatever they wanted in life, but I was never even asked.

The one time I told my father I wanted to be a teacher, he laughed. I'd been eager to tell him after seeing how he'd reacted to my two brothers sharing their ambitions. One wanted to join the army, and the other wanted to help him with the family business. I'd never been included in any talks about the family business to begin with.

In fact, the only time I'd ever come up in any conversation between my parents was to weigh my suitability to be married to particular men.

Ultimately, that's what led me to this train. My only purpose was to marry a man to help expand the influence of our family. Since I was disobedient, prone to argue, ungrateful, and all around unladylike, a lesson was needed.

A trip to my uncle's ranch was what they'd decided on. There, I'd learn to be grateful for my privileged life. I'd learn what hard work looked like and see the kind of life most women in this world had to live.

They supposed the shock of it all might unbind me from my stubbornness, and I'd happily go blindly serve the man chosen for me and eagerly bear his many children. Sons, God willing. What good woman would hope to burden her husband with daughters?

The train began slowly grinding to a halt, shaking me from my daydream. I was glad of the timing. Much longer, and I feared I'd join in the mad ramblings around me—either the old man spouting the glories of the war or the crying of the baby. It was hard to guess which one was the bigger waste of air.

Many of the passengers were eager to spill from the train, likely reuniting with lovers or relatives. Others settled in for their continued journey. I fought hard against the temptation of remaining in my seat and continuing on to wherever the train would take me. Though, the moment my father learned I hadn't arrived, I'd be tracked down like an outlaw and returned.

Some small part of me did look forward to this. It would be the first time I was truly apart from my family, so far away.

As most of the passengers paired up with their welcoming committee or set off on their own, I was able to study those who remained and determine who I was meant to depart with. I didn't know of any arrangements made in advance, so it was all guesswork. I would be able to learn a lot from the sort of man my uncle sent to fetch me—whether he was looking forward to my visit or if it was simply another of his brother's forced inconveniences.

Were I a gambling girl, my money would be on some drunkard.

As my eyes settled on one of the few remaining men waiting near the platform, I finally figured it out.

A cowboy, hastily dressed for the job in a half-hearted attempt to make himself look presentable. His hat was stained and dirty, just like most of the rest of him. He wore a button-up shirt, half-unbuttoned to the point he may as well have not been wearing one at all. His curly brown hair barely reached his ears, and he squinted in my direction in a way that made it impossible to determine his eye color.

One of the necessary worries of a woman was encountering a man too interested in her. This man could not be more disinterested in anything if he tried.

As he approached me, I knew the first thing he'd do was take my luggage, assuming I was too small and weak to carry it myself the short distance to the wagon, despite having handled it myself for the entirety of the trip.

Though, after a brief exchange of unpleasantries and half a dozen sighs from him, we managed to board the wagon he'd prepared and get moving. Even though I'd just told him it was unnecessary to make small talk with me, my curiosity eventually got the better of me.

"What's your name?" I asked.

"Does exchanging names count as small talk?" he replied, not even looking at me.

Somehow, his mirroring of my pettiness made me all the more aware of it. Though, I had plenty of reason to be petty and very little reason to be otherwise.

"Fine. I couldn't care less about your name."

"Funny you asked, then."

He turned and looked at me for the first time, grinning. Something about his grin felt especially off-putting. Like he had so many things to hide, but even worse, like he knew I was hiding something.

"Isn't it? You have quite a haughty disposition for a ranch hand. I wonder if you'd be so smug if I told my uncle you were rude to me."

"Smug!" he shouted, startling me. "That's the word I was thinking of. I couldn't remember it."

I narrowed my eyes at him. What sort of game was he playing?

"What are you talking about?"

"I was trying to think of a word to describe you, and it was on the tip of my tongue. Smug. That's the one."

"I'm not smug!" I said, my cheeks warming. I couldn't believe he'd say something like that.

What an annoying, ridiculous man. It was as though he'd never spoken to a woman in his life and had no idea how.

"Oh? Sorry, my mistake." He was briefly silent before sighing again. "Tom. To tell you the truth, I didn't even know you were coming or that I'd be picking you up until a few hours ago."

I finally caught a better look at his eyes as we passed beneath just the right angle of sunlight. A light hazel that almost looked golden in the glare.

"What does that have to do with anything?" I asked. "You were punctual enough."

"Now that sounds like a good thing to tell your uncle. I was punctual. After today, I doubt we'll need to speak to one another again."

I squeezed a handful of my dress into my fists as I held them firmly in my lap. This would be an embarrassing question, but my only opportunity to ask before arriving.

"What sort of man is my uncle?"

He shrugged, almost as though he didn't understand the question.

"How should I know? I'm not his niece."

I tilted my head, once again taken aback by his rudeness.

"What an odd thing to say."

"What an odd thing to ask," he replied. "Unless you plan on being a ranch hand."

We sat in silence for a good bit longer until the large arch came into view, welcoming us to Church Bell Ranch. I realized I'd never even asked the name.

"Do you have an issue with women, Tom?" I asked. Perhaps a question like this would get a direct answer.

"They're trouble. Is that what you mean?"

"Clearly, you've never been a woman," I said.

"I've never been a rattlesnake either."

Before I could catch myself, I sighed. He'd somehow made me stoop to his level. Something was clearly wrong with this man. I hadn't smelled any alcohol, but maybe he'd been drinking all the same. The sooner I could be rid of him, the better. I didn't know exactly why his presence irritated me so much, only that it did.

Fortunately, the ride had ended. My aunt and uncle were there to greet me.

Chapter Three

Tom Roland

I was more excited to see the welcome party than my young companion was. I was happy to be done with babysitting and back to less complicated work. I still didn't know the girl's name, despite giving her mine, but that was fine by me. I didn't really plan on getting to know her, and I certainly didn't want Marcus Henry thinking I was trying to. It helped that she seemed to hate my guts for some reason—another stroke of luck for me.

Mrs. Henry stepped forward as our wagon came to a stop by the front porch.

"Hello, Tabitha. How was the trip?"

As Mrs. Henry spoke, Mr. Henry came alongside her with a stool and an extended hand to help the young lady from the seat, shooting me a glare as he did.

I realized my mistake but didn't rush to correct it. Tabitha had already made it very clear she did not want nor need a man's assistance. I was more than happy not to provide it.

"Excuse Mr. Roland. He's more accustomed to labor than escorting ladies."

She batted his hand away gently, stepping off onto the stool without assistance, nearly falling as she did. She stood upright, quickly adjusting herself. "Well, you did send him, Uncle. So the choice reflects just as much on you as it does him. It doesn't matter, though. I can ride a horse or drive a carriage as well as any man."

I laughed, drawing even more glares. Mrs. Henry cleared her throat before anyone else could speak.

"Mr. Roland, would you mind bringing Tabitha's luggage upstairs?"

My heart sank. If I had to spend ten more minutes with this brat, I'd have to join the other men drinking later. There was no task I'd refuse if asked by Mrs. Henry, which I realized she was very aware of. She no longer told me to do anything. She just asked, as she did now, and I couldn't help but oblige. I couldn't risk that cold sassafras tea drying up.

I tipped my hat, stepping down from the wagon. Before I could close my hand around the handle of a suitcase, Mr. Henry put a hand on my shoulder and stopped me.

"Actually, Tom, I've got another job for you that can't really wait."

Thank goodness.

"Sure, Mr. Henry. What do you need?"

He seemed worried. Then again, Mr. Henry was a worrier—mostly over things that didn't require worrying… but not always.

"I need you to take a few of the men up to the northern property line. They're waiting for you at the stables. One of ours was up there earlier and found some of the new neighbors messing with the fence. Said they weren't too kind when he tried talking. I'd like you to talk to them and resolve the matter."

That was certainly odd.

"Oh… do we know anything about why they'd be up there? Their property isn't even all that big."

"Not a clue. I know you're not fond of guns, but you should probably carry one for your own safety."

I sighed but nodded along with the request. It would be foolish not to, though he was very correct that I wasn't all that fond of guns.

"How about I take the new guest with me? You want to ride out with us?" I said, turning to her with a grin.

"I…"

That caught her off guard, which I took pleasure in. It was the first time since she arrived that she didn't seem to know what to say.

"Tom Roland!" Mrs. Henry scolded. "Stop teasing the poor girl. She only just arrived, and you're making light of a very serious matter."

I laughed but was quick to calm the ranch matriarch. Mrs. Henry didn't anger often, and she wasn't at that point yet, but she was mean as a rattlesnake when she did.

"Apologies. Don't worry. I'm sure it's just some confusion about the property line. We'll get it cleared up, Mr. Henry."

Mr. Henry gave my shoulder a squeeze, my assurance seeming to lift his spirits a bit.

I tipped my hat to the young lady, clearly still irritated with me and as happy to be away from me as I was to be away from her. I made my way to the stables to meet up with the other men.

***

We rode out right away, knowing it would take us some time to get all the way up there. Mr. Henry owned well over a thousand acres and didn't exactly make use of it all. Much of the land ended up just being used for hunting—one of the perks of the job.

Despite the perks, the work was hard, and the turnover was high. Of the four men riding with me, I could only remember the name, or nickname, of two of them: Terrance Dempsy and a man they called Ditch. Ditch, on account of where his friends found him once nearly frozen to death. They hoped the nickname might discourage him from ending up in one again, and so far it seemed to have the intended effect. The other two? I'd talked to them a few times but couldn't remember their names for the life of me. After the first time, I hated asking again. I figured they wouldn't stick around long enough for it to matter anyway.

"Is it much further, Tom?" the youngest boy asked. He couldn't have been more than sixteen years old. The gun on his side flopped from his belt being too loose, and I wondered if his finger would be able to reach the trigger on that pistol even if he could manage to draw it—if the weight didn't tire out his arm before he could. Then again, we weren't going to war.

Hopefully…

"It's not much further," I said, slowing down.

My horse, Hooper, was a red chestnut mare—nothing special, at least at a glance. Didn't cost me a dime other than time and a lot of bruises. Mr. Henry had tried to sell her a few times, but she had a bad temperament for riding or just about anything else. It took a few months, but I wasn't about to look a gift horse in the mouth. Literally, in this case.

"Maybe give us a warning when you're going to stop like that. Not everyone's horse minds as well as yours does," Terrance said, struggling to get his own horse to slow.

"Yours just likes to run. That's all. Might come in handy today, but that's what I wanted to talk to all of you about. We're almost to the property line. Now… we don't know anything about these new neighbors. Maybe they're good folks. Maybe they like to drink and run their mouths. They'll probably have guns too. Last thing we need is a problem. Our problem becomes Mr. Henry's problem. Am I clear?"

The four men nodded, but I found myself wishing I'd just gone by myself and dealt with whatever consequences came of that.

We sped up again, and it wasn't long before we arrived. I was hoping the men would already be gone, but they were still here—three of them.

All three had pistols on their hips, and all three had rifles on their horses.

"Hello, gentlemen," I said, removing my hat as we rode up next to the partially dismantled fence.

They were bold to do something like this to Mr. Henry's property—bold and possibly impaired by the influence of alcohol.

"This here's private property," Terrance said as he dismounted. The rest of us followed suit.

The older man in front of us looked up from his digging, stroking his long, gray beard thoughtfully.

"Yeah, I reckon it is."

"Well, then you know who owns it," one of the young boys said.

I needed to work on my instructions, obviously, because they'd clearly not understood what I meant by avoiding a problem.

I held up my hand, hoping to signal my two coworkers to take it down a notch. At the same time, I slowly inched myself closer to the bearded man closest to me.

"We gonna have a problem?" a bearded man asked from the other side of the fence. He shared a similar look to the old man—a relative, for certain.

The moment he rested his hand on his pistol, I knew our problem had just become a lot bigger than a damaged fence…

Chapter Four

Tabitha Henry

"I'll help you get your luggage up to your room," Mr. Henry said, taking hold of the largest suitcase.

I simply smiled and nodded. I'd barely been here a few minutes and was already feeling smothered.

Before we could even take three steps inside, a man came stumbling in behind us, frantic.

"Sorry to bother you, Mr. Henry, but it looks like that cow's going into labor. Terrance was supposed to help me gather the tools and keep an eye on her, but he rode out with Tom and the others."

Mr. Henry was calm, but visibly irritated by the news.

"Didn't expect that for a few more days. Well… I really need to be here. I suppose I could ride out with you. How far out is she?"

"She went a ways out, Mr. Henry. She's near the edge of the pasture. That big oak tree down by the creek."

Mr. Henry rubbed his hands together, looking to his wife for guidance, but she only smiled in response. Her visible confidence in him seemed to bolster his own.

I saw my opportunity to experience something genuinely new today, and I wasn't about to let it pass me by.

"I'll go with him," I said.

Everyone looked at me as if I'd turned into a cow myself.

Mr. Henry hadn't outright denied my suggestion. He just scratched his beard and looked to his wife again, who only shrugged. I was beginning to feel that this happened often.

"Would that be alright?" Mr. Henry asked the man behind me.

He only seemed to become even more distressed at the suggestion.

"Well uh… if something goes wrong, it ain't exactly…"

Mr. Henry nodded, looking to me again and smiling. The same sort of smile you'd offer a child when attempting to explain something they aren't truly capable of understanding. I recognized the smile immediately and could feel myself becoming defensive before I even heard his words.

"Dear, maybe—"

"I'm aware there could be complications, my dress could be ruined, and I don't have any experience with this sort of thing. However, I'm not a child. All the same, I'd still like to go with him. I may be staying here a while. The sooner I'm exposed to the things that are a regular part of ranch life, the better. Right?"

I clenched my fists in frustration. Not at the situation, but at myself. I knew my reasoning was sound, but I could hear the entitlement in my own voice, and it made me self-conscious.

"Better than having nobody," the man said, shrugging his shoulders and offering me a reassuring smile.

I hated being appeased. I wanted to be taken seriously.

Mr. Henry simply nodded in agreement while still being unhappy with the unexpected circumstances we'd found ourselves in.

"That was my thinking, and it'll give my niece a chance to see the kind of things that happen here on the ranch. Just be careful."

I smiled, thankful I wore a more appropriate dress for the trip, against my mother's wishes, cut a little below the knee. I'd read they were more the style for girls in this part of the country and didn't want to show up looking like I was ready to attend a ball.

"Let's go!" I said, sounding much more excited than I intended.

***

The walk wasn't particularly far, but I was relieved when we reached the end of the pasture.

"It's already on the way out," the man said between short breaths. "Now, you and I really just need to stay out of the way unless something goes wrong. I got us a lantern and all the other things we might need, but I sure hope we don't need 'em. There's a log over there you can sit on and rest."

Reading about something and seeing it happen before your eyes are two very different things. I wasn't at all prepared for witnessing a live birth of any kind, but I was still determined to be just as calm as the cowboy.

"I've never seen a cow give birth before," I said.

"You don't say?" he replied dryly.

I wasn't sure if it was humor or irritation—maybe both. I guess in his shoes, I'd also be frustrated.

"As long as you tell me what to do, I can do whatever's needed," I said, trying not to sound too insistent. Failing, of course.

"It's alright, Ms. Henry. You can just watch," he said.

"But… I don't want to just watch. I'd like to be helpful if you need help. And you don't need to call me Ms. Henry. Tabitha is fine."

He didn't answer.

We watched for what felt like another hour, and it soon became apparent that this man did not want me here at all. He was just appeasing my uncle. I tried to make conversation a few more times but got grunts in response or was just outright ignored. At least the other man acknowledged me enough to be insulting.

Finally, after even more painful silence, the calf erupted from its mother.

The cowboy sighed in relief, which put me momentarily at ease. But it was only momentarily.

He took a step closer, leaning over and rubbing the calf's side roughly before shouting a curse that made me nearly jump out of my skin.

"What's wrong?" I said.

He sprinted over and grabbed a bucket he'd brought, dumping the random contents on the ground before making his way to the creek just a few feet away.

"What should I do?!" I shouted after him, but he didn't answer.

I dropped to my knees next to the calf, trying my best to remember what I'd read about complications. I had no idea what to do. In the tension of the moment, my mind was blank. I froze in silent panic. I knew I'd read about this. If I could just remember…

Yet, my body didn't move. A thousand thoughts filled my mind, but it felt like my brain disconnected from my muscles and any will to act. I could feel a sensation like I was floating outside my own body, observing myself sitting there, doing nothing and wondering why.

"Out of the way," he said as he ran back up the hill.

I thought I said something in reply, but I didn't.

"Out of the way!" he repeated, shouting this time as he shoved me aside, causing me to stumble and fall flat on my side in the grass a few feet away.

He tossed a bucket of water on the calf's head and it flinched. It was alive, at least.

The man shouted another curse and dropped to his knees, sticking his fingers in the calf's mouth and digging out mucus. In the next moment, he was on his feet, picking the small animal up by the back legs and swinging it from side to side. After a few seconds, he dropped it with a thud. The calf gasped and then started breathing normally.

I opened my mouth to say something but realized I couldn't. I was breathing too quickly and couldn't seem to catch my breath. I pivoted on my knees in the grass, turning my back to them.

Calm down. Calm down.

I repeated the words in my head over and over again until I at least had enough control to speak again.

"Are you hurt, Ms. Henry?" he asked.

I wasn't about to tell him the truth of the matter. I'd not only been useless, but I'd nearly stopped breathing myself.

"Please don't tell your uncle I shoved you. He'd have my hide if I let that calf go, but he'll be just as mad if you go back in tears. I need this job, Ms. Henry."

I just shook my head, waving my hands as I struggled back to my feet. I rubbed my eyes, only then realizing I'd been crying. I'd never been so embarrassed in my life. Then, embarrassment turned to frustration. Frustration to anger.

"You should have just told me what to do to help," I growled, swatting away his hand as he reached out to steady me.

Even as I said the words and meant them, I realized I would've been of no real help at all. If I'd just stood there, frozen, what exactly could I have done?

"Let's head back," he said, ignoring me once again. "The mother will take it from here."

I stomped back up the hill, feeling like this entire trip had been a horrible mistake and ashamed I'd ever looked forward to it.

Chapter Five

Tom Roland

Once men's tempers run hot, almost nothing in the world can cool them down. Egos come into play, and no man wants to be seen as the weaker. In my life, I'd realized just how many of my problems could've been solved or altogether avoided just by taking on the role of the weaker man in a conflict. It didn't always work, of course, but did surprisingly often.

Now, one might assume the young would be the most difficult to persuade when tensions are running high. Sometimes that was true, especially in a lone encounter. Young men haven't yet learned their limits, or come to terms with what they're willing to sacrifice for the paltry prize of feeling tough. Or, maybe having something to brag about to their friends later.

Yet, they weren't the worst. The worst was a man in the presence of those he valued the opinions of. Especially their opinions of him. Catch a man in front of a girl he wanted to impress, or a son in the presence of his father, and you've found yourself a man almost impossible to talk down. Far worse than a man compromising his opinion of himself is sacrificing the opinions others hold of him.

Without any meaningful hesitation, the bearded man nearest to me drew his pistol, but by now he was within arm's reach. My first instinct was to reach for the knife on my belt, but I fought it. It took more strength than I cared to give the man, but I convinced myself to reach for him with both hands empty.

When I pulled his wrist down, he struggled to get his thumb up to cock the hammer. I positioned my left hand to prevent just that.

Even with my attention elsewhere, I heard the familiar sound of guns clearing leather.

"Don't shoot!" I shouted. As I did, the man managed to cock the hammer and fire. I felt a burning shoot through my leg. The best I could tell, he'd hit me somewhere in the thigh. "Nobody shoot!" I repeated, even louder this time.

As I finally wrestled the gun from the man's grip, I heard Ditch's cracking voice behind me.

"Hurry and shoot, Terrance!" he shrieked.

"Holster your weapons! Stop!" I barked the orders as loudly as I could manage, throwing the bearded man's revolver on the ground as I did. I held my breath as I waited for the chaos to unfold. This was the deciding moment where gunfights started, and when they were avoided. If another shot was fired, most of us probably weren't going home.

To my great relief, only an uneasy silence followed. I fought against the pain in my leg, but also the rising anger.

"Are all of you really so stupid you're willing to die over a fence?" I growled through clenched teeth.

"It ain't in the right spot," the older man said before turning to the bearded man I'd just scuffled with. "Get that man something to put on his leg."

Reluctantly, the bearded man agreed, returning soon after with a spare shirt. Looked like the bullet had passed clean through the muscle, somehow avoiding the arteries. That much was obvious already, since I'd already be dead otherwise.

"What do you mean it's not in the right spot?" I countered.

"It's not. It's supposed to be along that big stone," the older man said, calmly pointing.

I strained my eyes, swiveling my head in every direction. I couldn't see any stone in the distance. I knew he couldn't mean the one right next to us.

"What stone?" I asked.

"That one."

He pointed again, and this time I followed his finger. He was actually pointing to the one right next to us, not three whole feet from the original fence.

"That one?" I pointed to the rock myself. I took a step toward it, intended to kick it, but the sharp pain that went through my leg stopped me. "You're talking about this rock right here? This one right next to us?"

I tried not to lose control and make things worse again. I couldn't believe a bunch of men nearly died over about two feet of fence.

"That's right," he said, firm. As silly as it seemed to me, it was a matter of principle to the old man. "That's what the deed states."

"And you're not contesting anything beyond this section? Just this short run of fence that passes by the stone?"

"That's right," he said again. To my surprise, he produced the deed from his back pocket, unfolding it and pointing to the section in question.

I did my best to ignore the pain surging through my leg, pressing the shirt against it. There was an exit wound, I was pretty sure, but I wasn't bleeding out so I didn't worry too much about it. If I had to, I was willing to spend a lot more time here to avoid riding back out again later. Today, the man was open to talking. Tomorrow, he might not be.

"Well…" I began, knowing what I was about to say might be a huge mistake that could cost me my job or more. "I'm reluctant to speak on behalf of Mr. Henry, but I'm pretty certain this is something he can live with. Like you said, it's plain as day in the deed. Mr. Henry can check his deed and see how things match up. Could be that whenever this fence was put up, they were just off a little bit. Things like that happen."

"Carter Richardson," he said, holding out his hand. I accepted it, giving him a firm handshake. "This here's my son, Anthony. If you want a doctor sent out, I'll be glad to cover the expense."

"Tom Roland. I appreciate the offer, Mr. Richardson, but it's just a flesh wound really. If anything, it might convince Mr. Henry to give me the rest of the day off."

"All the same, we're willing to make it right. Apologize, son."

Anthony Richardson took a step forward, removing his hat. Man had to be older than me, but took on the look of a toddler when scolded by his dad.

"Apologies, Mr. Roland."

I simply nodded in response. Last thing I wanted to do was encourage another back and forth when all I really wanted to do right now was get back to the ranch and take my weight off this leg.

"We done here, gentlemen?" I asked, looking around the group as I handed Mr. Richardson's deed back to him. "Any objections to what we just discussed?"

When no one immediately answered, I took the opportunity to return to my horse. After a bit of a struggle, I managed to mount her. I tipped my hat, and everyone else did the same, nearly at once.

The only thing that seemed to surpass these men's eagerness to get into a pointless gunfight was their relief at it having not happened. Plenty of irony there. I'd heard it said many times that men are simple creatures, but you don't hear us called smart nearly as often. For good reason.

"We could've beat them easy," Ditch said as we rode away, barely out of hearing distance.

"What's winning mean to you, Ditch?" I asked.

He didn't answer. I think my tone must've given away my frustration and hinted at my draining patience.

"How bad were you shot?" Terrance asked.

I wanted to make the joke that I'd been shot a lot more and a lot worse than this, but the truth in that made it much less of a joke.

"Looking forward to taking the day off tomorrow," I said. "I think I deserve it."

"Negotiating away part of Mr. Henry's property like that, I'm not sure he'll agree," said the young man I hadn't bothered to learn the name of.

"According to the man's deed, it ain't Mr. Henry's property," I said.

Again, no answer.

The remainder of the ride was dead silent.

Chapter Six
Tabitha Henry

Mr. Henry paced on the front porch, his temper short with anyone who beckoned him to take a seat in his rocking chair. The men who rode out had stayed out later than he'd expected, and he was very much a worrier. The only one who hadn't made any effort to try to calm him was his wife, and I followed her lead. Even though I'd not yet been here a full day, it was already clear to me that Mrs. Henry was the emotional anchor for my uncle, and perhaps for everyone here on the farm.

After being made painfully aware of my own emotional fragility, where I thought there'd been none, I found myself all the more impressed by her. At the same time, I was less judgmental of my pacing uncle.

"We're going to get a few lanterns and ride out there. They should've been back by now," he said.

"Now, dear, you know how Tom likes to talk. He probably saw the chance to spend his day chatting with the new neighbors instead of working, and did just that," Mrs. Henry replied in her usual, even tone.

He sighed, continuing his pacing but not pushing the matter to ride out himself just yet.

"Could've sworn I heard a gunshot earlier, but I couldn't hear it clearly."

"Surely if there was shooting, there'd be more than one shot," Mr. Williams said, joining the three of us on the porch. He hesitated, rubbing his beard before continuing. "And if you think you might've heard shots, do you think we should go get the sheriff before we ride out ourselves?"

My uncle stopped in his tracks momentarily, then ran his hand through his hair roughly as though this new option just added another burden to his already heavy mind.

"Maybe," he said, before continuing to pace. "Except that'll take a lot more time."

Before the discussion could go further, we spotted several men riding in from the distance. My uncle quickly rushed off the porch to meet them, doing his best to appear as though he wasn't in a hurry. He stopped just at the bottom of the stairs.

"Took you long enough," he said.

"Yeah, well, Tom was awfully busy giving away a piece of your property to the new neighbor," Terrance said as he dismounted, tying his horse off.

"Shut up, Terrance. Nobody asked you," Tom said.

Terrance looked annoyed but thought better of saying anything else, at least not without my uncle to back him up. The two other men had stayed quiet from the start and seemed eager to depart.

"It was just a few feet of fence, and his deed did back up his claim. I'm not thrilled to be speaking on your behalf, but I figured you'd value these men's lives over a couple of feet of fence on a twenty- or thirty-foot stretch."

Mr. Henry nodded.

"I trust you to be level-headed. That's why I sent you. We'll have to compare deeds to make it official, but he—" When Tom got off the horse, he stumbled, and my uncle grabbed his arm to steady him. He looked down and saw the blood. "Jesus, Tom! What happened?"

"This here? Don't worry too much about that, Mr. Henry. It's just a flesh wound. The conversation may have ended cordially, but it certainly didn't start out that way."

"Do you want me to have someone fetch the doctor? It won't hurt to have it looked at."

Tom stepped back, seemingly offended. "No. Like I said, it ain't much more than a scratch. I'll put a bandage on it, and it'll be good by morning."

I wanted desperately to say something, but after the experience earlier today with the calf, I found myself lacking the confidence to speak up. He needed to be seen by a doctor. Surely everyone knew that. By morning, he could have a serious infection.

Mr. Henry sighed. "If you say so, Tom. I won't force the matter. I know how much you dislike doctors."

Tom limped toward the bunkhouse, waving off Mr. Williams's offer to help. The other men dispersed quickly, clearly eager to distance themselves from whatever consequences might follow their afternoon's adventure. Only Terrance lingered, shooting Tom dark looks that my uncle thankfully didn't notice.

"Terrance, go see to the horses," Mr. Henry said, his tone showing enough deteriorating patience to end any desire to argue further. At least for now.

As Tom disappeared into the bunkhouse, I found myself staring after him longer than I should have. The man was infuriating, stubborn, and had spent our entire wagon ride making me feel foolish. So why did I feel this strange irritation in my stomach as I watched him limp away, clearly in more pain than he was willing to admit? I guess I didn't just feel foolish. I very much was foolish.

"Tabitha, dear, would you help me with supper?" Mrs. Henry asked, though it sounded more like a gentle command than a request.

I nodded, grateful for something to occupy my hands and mind. Following her into the kitchen, I tried to push away the image of Tom stumbling as he dismounted, the dark stain spreading across his pant leg, and the sight of the poor calf struggling to take its first breaths while I stood there doing nothing.

Mrs. Henry handed me a wooden spoon and pointed toward a large pot simmering on the stove. "Just stir that occasionally. Don't let it stick to the bottom."

I took the spoon, focusing on the simple task. The kitchen was warm and filled with the comforting scents of whatever Mrs. Henry had been preparing. It reminded me of our cook back home, though I'd never been allowed to help in the kitchen there. According to my mother, only poor ladies cooked.

"You look troubled," Mrs. Henry observed, not looking up from the bread she was slicing.

"I'm fine," I said automatically, then caught myself. After today's events, I was beginning to question whether I was fine about anything. "Actually, no. I'm not fine. That man needs to see a doctor. Anyone can see that."

Mrs. Henry smiled. "Tom's seen worse, I'm sure. Probably more than Marcus and I know about."

"That's not the point. Even the toughest men can die from infections."

"I get that you're worried, but trying to convince a man like that will just make him dig his heels in even more."

It wasn't a question whether the man needed medical attention, but how quickly he needed it. That it was even up for discussion made heat rise in my cheeks. I didn't know why I should feel embarrassed for stating the obvious. "I'm worried about anyone who's too stubborn to seek proper medical care. Uncle should insist."

"Mmm. Maybe." Mrs. Henry's response was noncommittal, but I caught the slight curve of her lips. It felt a bit condescending.

I stirred the pot more vigorously than necessary. "He was rude to me today. Insufferably rude."

"Yes, I imagine he was."

"Then why would I care if he—" I stopped myself, realizing how my voice had risen. "Maybe a terrible infection would serve him right."

Mrs. Henry set down her knife and looked at me directly. "Tabitha, caring about someone doesn't require liking everything about them. I'm sure most doctors dislike many of their patients. You don't have to feel embarrassed about being compassionate."

I opened my mouth to protest, but the words died in my throat. Was I worried about Tom? He'd made it clear he found me bothersome.

"The man's ill-mannered. It's his choice if he wants to die from stubbornness," I said finally.

"If you say so, dear."

Her tone suggested she didn't believe me for a second, which was particularly irritating because I wasn't entirely sure I believed myself.

A knock at the back door interrupted my spiraling thoughts. Mrs. Henry wiped her hands on her apron and opened it to reveal one of the young ranch hands I'd seen earlier.

"Begging your pardon, Mrs. Henry, but Tom's asking if you might have some clean bandages."

Mrs. Henry glanced at me, then back at the young man. "Of course. Tabitha, would you take some supplies to him? I need to finish supper."

My heart jumped. "I don't think that's appropriate. We barely know each other, and there are implications for a man and a woman having that kind of contact."

"Nonsense. You're family, and he's injured. Besides, I'm sure he'd appreciate some help in tending the wound properly. You can… how did you put it? Insist."

Before I could protest further, Mrs. Henry had gathered clean cloth, a bottle of something that smelled strongly of alcohol, and a small jar of what looked like salve. She pressed them into my hands along with a basin of warm water.

"Just clean it properly and bandage it tight. And if you're determined, don't let him argue with you about it."

A few minutes later, I found myself standing outside the bunkhouse door, supplies in hand. Through the thin walls, I could hear Tom moving around inside, accompanied by occasional muttered curses that made me grateful for my limited exposure to such language—language my father always told me was common among lesser men.

I knocked hesitantly.

"What?" came his gruff response.

"It's… it's Tabitha. Mrs. Henry sent me with supplies for your wound."

A long pause.

"I can handle it myself."

"Well, clearly you can't, or you wouldn't have asked for bandages."

Another pause, longer this time. I was beginning to think he'd simply ignore me when the door opened.

Tom stood in the doorway, his shirt removed and a mostly bloody cloth pressed against his thigh. In the lamplight, I could see the wound clearly for the first time—a dark hole in his leg that was still seeping blood. My stomach lurched. I'd never seen a gunshot wound before, and I felt instantly lightheaded.

"You look like you're about to pass out," he observed, holding out his hand. "Give me those and head back to the house."

The dismissive tone in his voice sparked something in me. After my embarrassing performance with the calf earlier, I wasn't about to prove him right about my supposed weakness.

"Move aside," I said, pushing past him into the small room.

The bunkhouse was sparse but clean—just a bed, a small table, and a washstand. Tom's few possessions were neatly arranged, giving the space an almost military orderliness that surprised me.

"Sit down," I commanded, setting the supplies on the table.

"I can—"

"Sit. Down." I used the same tone I'd heard Mrs. Henry employ earlier when she wanted no arguments.

To my amazement, Tom complied, lowering himself onto the edge of the bed with a grimace. He kept the bloody cloth pressed to his leg, watching me warily as I arranged the bandages and salve.

"This is probably going to hurt," I warned, dampening a clean cloth with the alcohol.

"Won't be the first time."

There was something in his voice—a resignation that spoke of experience with pain far beyond what any normal laborer should have endured. I found myself curious about his past, about what had brought him to this place, but I pushed the questions aside. I certainly didn't want to give him any impression that my interest extended anywhere beyond his wound.

"Remove your hand," I said.

He hesitated, then slowly lifted the makeshift bandage away. The wound was worse than I'd thought—not just a graze, but a proper bullet hole that had passed clean through the muscle. Blood welled up immediately, even hours later. Then again, he hadn't stayed off it properly, of course.

I pressed the alcohol-soaked cloth against it without warning. Tom's sharp intake of breath was the only sign he gave of the pain, though I noticed his knuckles go white where he gripped the edge of the bed.

"Sorry," I murmured, working as quickly as I could to clean the wound. "It has to be done properly, or…"

"Or I'll die of infection," he finished. "I know."

Despite his gruff exterior, he held perfectly still while I worked, making my task easier. As I cleaned away the dried blood, I found myself stealing glances at his face. Without his usual scowl, he looked younger somehow, though still weathered by sun and hard work. And whatever else life had thrown at him.

"There," I said finally, applying the salve as gently as I could. "Now the bandage."

Wrapping the clean cloth around his thigh required me to get quite close to him, and I was acutely aware of his presence and his distinctly masculine scent. I could practically hear my mother's voice in my head scolding me about how inappropriate this was. My hands trembled slightly as I tied off the bandage, and I hoped he didn't notice.

"You did good," he said quietly as I gathered up the soiled cloths. "I expected you to pass out."

The unexpected praise caught me off guard. "I'm not that delicate."

"Could've fooled me."

I looked up to find him watching me with an expression I couldn't quite read. For a moment, the antagonism between us seemed to find an uneasy truce.

"You should have a doctor look at it tomorrow," I said.

"We'll see."

I knew that was the best answer I was likely to get from him. Clearly, he did not intend to and only wanted to avoid the lecture. Standing up, I moved toward the door, then paused.

"Tom?"

"Yeah?"

"That was good of you, what you did today. Preventing bloodshed, I mean."

He was quiet for so long I thought he wouldn't respond. Finally, he sighed. "Men are too eager to die. Sometimes for nothing at all."

The seriousness of his tone caught me off guard, and once again I sensed a story behind it. Still, I had the feeling I'd already overstayed my welcome.

Chapter Seven

Tom Roland
Two Months Later

"Tom Roland, you are the most stubborn man I've ever met!" Tabitha shouted from the ground below, looking up at me with an almost inhuman rage. Whatever motherly spirit possessed this young woman, I prayed every day for it to be exorcised.

"Won't even take another hour. Don't you have something better to do than bother me?" I shouted back, not looking up from my work on the barn's roof.

She'd managed to talk the other two men down nearly an hour ago, but the way I see it, I work for Mr. Henry. Not his brat niece.

"A man died in this heat not three days ago. Are you stupid?"

"Yep!" I casually shouted in reply. "Dumber than a box of steel rocks in a thunderstorm, my daddy always used to say."

"Your daddy did not say that!"

"He sure did…" I continued hammering. "If you distract me and make me fall off this roof, you'll feel awfully guilty."

Her face went as red as mine, and I was badly sunburned. She clenched both fists tightly at her sides and stomped hard enough for me to hear all the way up on the roof. She growled, sounding more beast than woman, before storming off. About time. Maybe I could get this done sooner now that there was some peace and quiet.

I had to pause to wipe the sweat out of my eyes, making my vision blurry. The sun's rays felt like a grinding stone on my blisters. Maybe the girl was right, but there was no way I could admit that now. Give an inch, they take a mile. This brat was already on my case enough.

She reappeared before I could clear all the sweat from my eyes, and I felt something impact the side of the barn, not quite reaching the roof. Another growl from the little lady, and the next throw made it up.

"Throwing stuff at me isn't going to make me get down any sooner," I said casually.

"I soaked a towel in water. At least cool yourself down with it!" She paused, unable to contain her emotions. "Idiot! Stupid man!"

I sighed, picking up the towel. At this point, the roof felt like a safer place to be. The moment the cool water touched my skin, a wave of relief washed over my whole body. It was one of the best feelings I'd ever experienced in my life. I draped it around my neck and continued working.

"Thanks…" I said, reluctant to give her any praise she might interpret as encouragement. "Now go find something else to do."

Without answering, she stomped away, still angry with me for reasons I couldn't quite understand. She'd been a pain in my rear since the moment she got here, and I was well past my patience wearing thin. Still, she was the boss's precious little niece, and I found the reserves to keep bearing it.

Terrance appeared over the top of the roof, climbing up the ladder on the other side.

"Your mother really is something else. Only man I know with a mother younger than him."

I laughed, sliding the bucket of nails toward him so we both could reach it.

"She ain't just like that with me. She's a pain, is what she is. Wish Mrs. Henry would make her help out with the chores more so we could have some peace during the day."

Terrance shook his head, taking a nail from the bucket and hammering another shingle into place.

"You like to antagonize her a bit too, Tom. The rest of us were happy to have an excuse to take a break and cool off. Normally, you would be too. Passing up a chance to slack off just ain't like you. I think you're doing it to spite the poor girl."

I stopped my hammering and looked up at Terrance. "Oh, is that right? You're dangerously close to calling me lazy."

"Yeah? Dangerously close to telling the truth, then."

"That's a hurtful thing to say to a man that's been up here roofing alone for close to an hour in the summer heat."

"I think I know your problem," Terrance said, resuming his hammering. "Anybody starts talking to you about anything other than what we're doing, you start getting smart. You know, they say sometimes a man gets like that when his mother didn't hug him enough."

I turned my gaze downward, resuming my own hammering. "I'm told my mother was someone who liked to give a lot of hugs to her kids."

"Told? Oh…"

"Right, passed away from a fever when I was a baby. My daddy and older sister took care of me, though she wasn't much more than a kid herself."

"I was just foolin' with that talk. Sorry, Tom. I didn't know that about your mother."

"Well, I shared something about myself, so now you can't claim I never do. Now, how about we get this roof finished before supper?"

Terrance nodded, too embarrassed to say more.

Truth is, I just said all that to shut the man up. I didn't know a single thing about my mother and wouldn't reveal it if I did.

I could at least thank the woman, whoever she was and wherever she was, for helping me change the topic. It wasn't that I didn't ask my daddy about her, but the anger in his voice whenever I did broke me of that habit real quick.

"Looks like we'll still be done by sundown," he said. "Mrs. Henry put on a big ol' pot of soup beans with some hog we slaughtered the other day. Now that woman knows how to cook."

"I wish her niece would spend more time learning from the woman instead of pestering the men out here."

Terrance grinned, speeding up his pace, maybe a little too much. "I reckon she's one of those women who wishes she was born a man while havin' no clue what the life of bein' a man actually is."

"Me and you don't know what bein' a woman's like either, Terrance. Why don't you slow it down a bit? It ain't like those soup beans are going to disappear if we're ten minutes late to dinner, but if we have to come back up here after the next rain and fix something, neither one of us is going to be happy about it."

He slowed his pace, but only a little. "You don't know that, Tom. Last time you said that, we ended up not getting any dinner at all, much less cold."

"Just keep hammering, big guy, and we might not even be late."

"You just told me to slow down! Tom, you're just as bad as Little Miss Henry."

"Twice as pretty. Now come on, let's—"

I paused, spotting several men riding in from the distance. Lawmen, by the look of it.

"Now if there's one thing you can't fault the girl on, it's her looks." He followed my gaze. "Looks like a few deputies. If you want to head down there and see what they need, I'll finish up here."

I didn't answer, just kept watching them. I heard him but barely registered a word he said.

He waved his hand in front of my face.

"Hey, Tom, you in there? I said you can head—"

"You go take care of it. I can't stand those men," I said, grabbing another shingle and hammering away.

"Scared of hard work, scared of guns, scared of doctors, and now you're scared of lawmen too?"

My stomach was in knots. "Well, maybe there's a reason I became a ranch hand. Not every man has to be some famous gunslinger."

"Yeah, yeah… fair enough," Terrance said, tossing his hammer on the roof and backing toward the ladder. "At least I won't have to worry about missing the soup beans."

"Be a pal and set a bowl back for me. Least you can do dipping out of the job early."

Terrance narrowed his eyes at me as he disappeared over the edge. I took a deep breath, and then several more.

Last thing I wanted to deal with today.

Chapter Eight

Tabitha Henry

"I wonder what those deputies want," my aunt said, pulling back the curtain in the kitchen and peering out. Nothing ever escaped this woman's notice.

"Hopefully nothing bad," I said, so focused on the pie crust I was struggling with that I hadn't even noticed them riding up in the first place.

"I'm going to join Marcus and see what they have to say. While I'm gone, you head out to the cellar and get a few cans of beans," she said, dropping the curtain and heading toward the front door without waiting for my response.

Exactly the opposite of what I was hoping she'd say. By now, I'd regained my confidence, and with it returned my irritation with my situation. And the men here, who seemed to share a single brain among the lot.

Still, I'd learned a lot from my aunt in the past couple of months. I now knew my way around the kitchen pretty well, considering I'd never been allowed to touch anything in my very fancy one back home. I was also in awe of how she seemed to always know exactly what to say and do in every situation. She was as level-headed as any man under stress, and, unlike me, everyone listened to her and followed her advice. If she put her foot down, no one argued. Even though she had never produced children of her own, it was as though she was everyone's mother.

As much as I wanted to be nosy, if she asked me to go fetch green beans, that's what I would do.

Heading out the back door, the only person in sight was the incredibly stubborn Mr. Roland, who had become the most insufferable of all. It was for that reason I never understood why my uncle called him 'the most reliable man on the ranch' when I asked why he kept a man like that around. Reliably unreliable, perhaps. No respect for women, save for my aunt, and very little for anyone else. He could never be found when you needed him for work, yet refused to take breaks when you didn't want him to work. It was as if the man had fashioned his entire existence to spite me.

He regarded me with a brief nod before returning to the roofing, and I simply turned my head away in response. I could see the man's sunburns from here.

Opening the cellar door, I stepped down, enjoying the cool air that hit me as I descended deeper. After browsing a few of the shelves directly in front of me, I picked up a glass jar of green beans and studied the seal on top.

That was when I felt a hand grip my mouth and the unmistakable feeling of a knife against my neck. It burned as I felt the blade break skin, and a line of blood run down my neck. I was frozen, unable to speak or move, and utterly terrified of what might follow.

"Don't say a word. You scream, I slice that pretty neck of yours wide open."

I nodded, fighting back the tears already forming in my eyes.

My mind flooded with all the possibilities, which only seemed to paralyze me even more. As he pulled me back, my legs barely held me up.

"Walk," he growled. "You must be the farmer's daughter, huh? A ranch owner could pay pretty good money to get his sweet little girl back unharmed."

I knew then it wasn't one of the ranchers. This man was a stranger, and I had the presence of mind to piece things together. The deputies that showed up. This was probably an escaped outlaw. My blood ran colder than the draft from the cellar. A man like this had nothing to lose and wouldn't think twice about hurting anyone. Or worse.

I nodded, stepping slowly up the stairs as he turned me around. I tried to get a glimpse of his face in the glass of a jar as we passed, but it was impossible in the dim lighting that came in from the cellar door.

I prayed that someone, anyone, might see us and help. I saw a glimpse of Mr. Roland as we exited, but I was certain he hadn't seen us. I looked around and saw no one else. They'd all gone to the front of the house to speak to the deputies. I turned back toward the barn, hoping to signal Mr. Roland in some way, only to find he'd disappeared into thin air. Typical of the man. Now he takes a break, of all times, or he'd more likely ended his work for the day to join everyone for supper. They'd notice I was gone soon, but by then this man would have dragged me off to who knows where. My tears ran freely now. There was no one to help me. I'd never been so terrified in my entire life.

I found myself missing the sheltered life I had before, and my father's guards. All the servants watching me like hawks. Nothing like this would've ever happened at home. I was a prisoner there too, or a marriage token, but this was worse. No matter what this man had planned for me, all of it was worse.

I considered risking it all and screaming, but he sensed my growing boldness and pressed the knife harder against my throat again, clamping his hand down hard enough over my mouth that my teeth cut into my lips. I thought for a moment he might break my front teeth from the sheer pressure of his hand.

"Don't even think about screaming. You hear me? Nobody here can run quick enough to stop you from bleeding out. I killed a woman and two men already, and I've got no problem adding you. Play your cards right, and you won't get hurt. I'll need your daddy to pay up, after all."

I nodded again, panic setting in as we entered the thick cornfield. After a few steps in, no one would see us, and maybe no one would see me ever again. We continued on for a few seconds longer, then stopped. The man tensed, and I wondered if he had stepped on a snake. Whatever it was, he didn't move a muscle.

"You feel that?" A different man's voice said. "Turn around, and I'll put a hole right through you. Trust me, I've got no problem shooting a man like you in the back."

It sounded familiar, but in my panic, I couldn't place it. The man holding me hesitated for a moment, but then I felt his grip loosen and the knife slowly move away from my neck. I stumbled a few steps forward, then turned. He was wearing a bandana over his face, but I recognized him easily. It was Mr. Roland. He held his finger to his lips, stopping me as I was about to scream for help.

My kidnapper saw this as his chance and quickly turned with his knife swinging as he did. Before he could turn halfway around, a hammer caught him in the head, and he crumpled to the ground.

I covered my mouth and took another step back. In two big steps, Mr. Roland was standing in front of me, squeezing my shoulders hard enough to cause me pain. For a moment, I thought I heard him asking me if I was alright. Maybe that's what I was hoping he'd ask or expecting.

"You want to thank me? Here's how. I wasn't here. Got it? You had a chance to pick up the hammer as he was dragging you away, then when the man was distracted by something he heard, you hit him as hard as you could. Count to a hundred, then scream. They'll all come running except me. We clear?"

My mind raced, trying to understand what was happening. The bandana to hide his face, demanding I pretend he didn't save me, that he wasn't here.

"Is… is he dead?" I asked, unable to take my eyes away from the blood pooling beneath him on the ground. I wasn't sure why I asked that. It wasn't the most pressing thing on my mind.

"Are we clear?" he repeated, his anger startling me as much as the shake that came with it.

I nodded.

"We're clear. You're hurting me, Mr. Roland."

He let go instantly, as though he'd touched a hot stove, then left. I did just as he asked, counting slowly to a hundred before screaming as loud as I could. I picked up the hammer and clutched it tightly to my chest.

Chapter Nine

Tom Roland

"Where were you the whole time, Tom?" Mr. Henry shouted, shoving me backward a few steps.

"Sorry, Mr. Henry. I'd been up on that hot roof all day, and when I finally went to take a break in the barn, I guess I fell asleep."

"You fell asleep so hard that you didn't hear a woman scream… and you were gone over an hour. We started to wonder if one of them had dragged you off somewhere too," Buster said.

The deputies had already left, satisfied with collecting the man they were looking for and having no other reason to stick around. Much to my relief.

"What do you want me to say, Buster? I'm sorry. It's not like I heard and just didn't help on purpose. Just bad timing."

Mr. Henry opened his mouth to speak again, and something about the angry look on his face told me I had yet to get the worst of it. My best guess was he was about to fire me. However, before he could speak, Tabitha grabbed his arm.

"Please, Uncle. Let's stop fighting about this. It wasn't Tom's fault. I just really want to sit down and have dinner right now. All of us."

"But—"

"Marcus Henry, that is enough," Mrs. Henry said, her voice firm but calm. Her tone didn't leave any room for argument. Not even from the proud Mr. Henry.

Mr. Henry's expression softened almost instantly as he glanced at his family and all the ranch hands present. After a moment, he sighed, nodded, then turned back toward the house. He motioned for all of us to follow as he walked.

I knew the worst wasn't over. Tabitha wouldn't let this go, and the questions would come pouring in sooner or later. For now, the poor girl seemed shaken up enough that interrogating me could wait. Seeing someone die will do that to a person. Especially the first time it happens. Less so with the second, and so on.

"You're lucky Mr. Henry didn't flog you with a whip for that one, Tom," Buster said, walking close to me, speaking low enough that the others couldn't hear.

I couldn't tell if he was relieved it didn't come to that or disappointed.

"Can't say I'd blame the man for it. If that was your niece, wouldn't you?"

"I hope the girl handles things alright," he said, ignoring my question.

"She'll be alright eventually. Ain't that the way it is with everything?"

Buster shook his head, a faint smile forming on his lips.

"Depends on what you call alright, Tom. Sure, the hurt of something can go away over time, but the changes it makes in a person stick around. Some things stay with you the rest of your life. Like being whipped, come to think of it. When I'm old and gray, I reckon that'll still be with me."

It was easy to forget that Buster was born and raised a slave… especially considering how much he liked telling everyone what to do. Going from being a slave to being a foreman was a big change, but one Buster adjusted to with no effort.

"Yeah, I suppose that would stick with a man. Lots of things do."

He responded with only a grunt and a nod, having said everything he wanted to on the matter. Though I knew full well it wasn't luck. If Tabitha hadn't stepped in, I'd be packing my things right now instead of heading to dinner.

Can't say she didn't owe me one for saving her life.

***

Dinner was quieter than usual. Mrs. Henry had outdone herself with the soup beans and cornbread, but most of us just pushed food around our bowls. Even the younger hands, who usually chattered and boasted through meals, seemed to understand this wasn't the time for their usual antics.

Tabitha sat directly across from me but kept her eyes fixed on her bowl. She'd barely touched her food, which wasn't lost on Mrs. Henry.

"Tabitha, dear, you've barely eaten anything," Mrs. Henry observed, her voice gentle with concern. "I know you've been through a lot today, but you should at least fill your belly."

"I'm fine, Aunt Jane. Just not very hungry."

"I understand. Maybe you should rest early tonight."

"Maybe." Tabitha's voice was distant, like her mind was somewhere else entirely.

Mr. Henry cleared his throat. "I've decided we're going to post an armed guard at night for the next few weeks. Just until we're certain there aren't any other… undesirables in the area."

"That's wise," Buster agreed. "I can take the first watch tonight."

"No need for that," I said, perhaps too quickly. "I'll take first watch."

Killing, no matter the number of notches on the belt or the cause, never made for an easy rest. At least not the first night.

"That's good of you, Tom," Mr. Henry said, though his tone suggested he was still very much angry with me.

I kept my mouth shut and continued eating. No point in making things worse by saying anything. What could I say?

Terrance broke the silence. "Lucky thing that hammer was lying around where you could reach it, Miss Henry. Could've been a lot worse if you hadn't been quick-thinking."

Tabitha nodded without looking up. "Yes. Very lucky. I'm thankful to Tom for letting it slide off the roof earlier."

I could hear something strained in her voice, but the others seemed to take her at face value. She was sticking to the story, just like she'd agreed.

"Takes real courage to do what you did," Buster added. "Most folks would've been too scared to think straight. Not sure I'd have been half as brave."

"I was scared," she said quietly. "Terrified, actually."

"But you kept your head anyway. I've never met your maw, but you sure are a Henry woman through and through."

Tabitha finally looked up, but her eyes found me instead of Buster. There was something in her expression I couldn't quite place. Not anger, exactly, but… questions. Lots of them, I had a feeling.

"Sometimes you just do what you have to do," she said, still looking at me. "And no one should feel ashamed of that."

Mr. Henry reached over and squeezed his niece's hand. "I'm proud of you, Tabitha. And grateful you're safe. You need anything, you just let anybody here know."

She turned to him and managed a small smile. "Thank you, Uncle. That means a lot."

The conversation moved on to other things: the repairs still needed on the barn, plans for the next day's work, speculation about whether the weather would hold. Normal ranch talk that helped ease the tension in the room.

But I could feel Tabitha's eyes on me throughout the meal, even when I wasn't looking directly at her. She was thinking hard about something, and that made me nervous. The girl was too smart for her own good, and definitely too smart for mine. Thinking I'd ever be able to stave off her curiosity for good was a fool's errand, but I couldn't just watch the girl get dragged off.

When dinner ended, the men began to file out. Some nodded their goodnights, others just headed for the bunkhouse or their evening chores without a word. I started to follow, but Mrs. Henry's voice stopped me.

"Tom, would you mind helping Tabitha carry the dishes to the kitchen? I need to speak with Marcus about something."

Before I could make an excuse, she and Mr. Henry had disappeared into the front room, leaving me alone with Tabitha and a table full of dirty dishes. Not that I'd have given Mrs. Henry any excuses anyway.

We worked in silence for a few minutes, stacking bowls and gathering utensils. But I could feel the weight of unasked questions hanging between us like a storm cloud.

Finally, as we carried the last of the dishes into the kitchen, she spoke.

"You're not going to tell me what really happened out there, are you?"

I set the dishes down by the washbasin and turned to face her. "You know what happened. You were there."

"I was there." She crossed her arms, studying my face. "But there are things that don't make sense."

"Such as?"

"Such as why you had a bandana covering your face. Such as why you don't want anyone to know you helped me."

I leaned against the counter, trying to look casual despite the knot forming in my stomach. "Maybe you were just confused. Scared. Sometimes our minds play tricks on us when we're in danger."

She shook her head. "My mind wasn't playing tricks, Tom. You saved my life, and for some reason, you don't want credit for it. You're modest but not that modest. Why?"

I looked out the kitchen window, watching the last light fade from the sky. How could I explain? It was simple. I couldn't.

"Some things are better left alone," I said finally. "So leave it alone."

"Is that your answer for everything? Just leave it alone?"

"It's my answer for this. Don't you owe me that much?"

She was quiet for a long moment, and I thought maybe she was going to let it go. But then she stepped closer, lowering her voice.

"I meant what I said earlier. Thank you. Whatever your reasons… I'll respect that. But I won't forget what you did."

The gratitude in her voice made something twist uncomfortably in my chest. I wasn't used to being thanked, especially not by her.

"Just stick to the story," I said. "That's all the thanks I need."

She nodded, but I could tell this conversation wasn't over in her mind. It was just postponed, and maybe not for long. Normally, seeing a man killed before your eyes was enough to shut down your logic for a day or two, but that was apparently not true of Tabitha Henry.

And that worried me more than any outlaw with a knife ever could.

Chapter Ten

Tabitha Henry

I stood at my bedroom window for a long while, looking out over the vast wilderness that stretched from my uncle's property. Despite the performance I'd put on, I was not in the state of mind for sleep. Not this night, and perhaps not even the next.

The image replayed in my mind over and over: Tom's hammer coming down and striking the man in the head, the way he fell to the ground, the look on his face as his final breaths escaped. I could've gone my whole life without seeing a man die, and now that I had, it was something I'd never be able to unsee.

At moments, I even wondered if Tom might have somehow avoided it, but there was no way that would happen without risking his own life and mine. He'd already tried to fool the man with the wooden handle of his hammer. He wouldn't have worn a bandana if he'd planned to kill the man from the start. No… Tom had intended to scare him off.

I'd stood there thinking of myself, but I'd failed to consider what Tom might be going through right now. He seemed okay, but everyone thought I was as well. I wasn't okay.

I paced from one end of my room to the other, toying with one of the curls of my blonde hair. I'd taken my hair down, but hadn't bothered undressing.

It would be inappropriate to go to him right now, wouldn't it?

Then again, since when have I cared about propriety?

I opened my door as quietly as I could, moving carefully down the stairs and out the front door.

Tom turned his head only partway to confirm the identity of the person coming out, then fixed his gaze forward again. The rifle sat lazily in his lap, as though he might not even realize it was there. He rocked slowly back and forth in the rocking chair, and I stood in front of the empty one beside him.

"May I join you, Mr. Roland?" I asked.

He did not answer. He only nodded, not bothering to look at me as he did.

I sat, opening my mouth to speak, only to find I hadn't prepared the words in advance and was therefore unable to say anything. I closed my mouth, relaxing in my chair to mirror his calm demeanor, and chose instead to sit in silence with him for several minutes before giving it another try.

"You have some idea of what I want to ask, don't you?" I said, as though I were a deputy about to begin my interrogation. I realized my tone and immediately felt embarrassed. "Not that you have to tell me anything."

"Nope," he replied, still not looking at me.

"Do you mean you don't know what I'm going to ask, or that you're not going to answer?" I asked, smiling, trying to lighten the mood.

"Let's go with both," he said.

"Mind if I make some guesses then?"

Tom sighed, looking at me for the first time since I'd joined him. "You know what? Let's hear them. It'll kill the time."

"You're an outlaw, aren't you?" I asked. The question itself felt dangerous, but what kind of man would hurt a woman he'd just saved, even if the question was out of line?

"You're bold to ask a man holding a rifle that, all alone," he said, laughing quietly.

"I'm not scared of you, Tom. And it isn't because I'm brave. It's because you're a kind man, in spite of your stubbornness."

His expression shifted immediately, and his grip tightened on the rifle in his lap, enough to turn his knuckles white in the lantern light. He looked away, but not before I glimpsed the pain in his expression. Why had he laughed at being accused of being an outlaw, but recoiled so strongly at being called kind?

"You don't know me," he said. The words sounded halfway between the growl of an animal and the strained voice of a child trying not to cry.

"I'm sorry," I said, clutching at the fabric of my dress in my lap. Communicating with people was never my best skill. "But that's what I believe."

"Go back inside," he said.

"No," I snapped back.

"Look, just leave me alone. Ever consider maybe I offered to do the first watch because I want to be by myself?"

"I'm not leaving," I said again, crossing my arms.

He laughed. "Right, and I'm stubborn. I'm the stubborn one. Okay, fine. If you insist on sitting out here and bothering me, tell me what it was like to grow up as a rich kid. I'd like to experience it second-hand."

It was meant to cut me, to frustrate me into leaving and going back inside. Instead, I took advantage of the opening to give him exactly what he asked for and stay.

"When I was little, I had a really great teacher. Ms. Yates. I looked up to her so much that I decided I wanted to be a teacher too. I must've been about eight years old at the time, so she probably thought it was a cute thing for a child to say and nothing more. Kids say those sorts of things all the time about what they want to be when they grow up."

Tom nodded and seemed to be listening attentively, which surprised me. I half-expected him to get angry and insist again that I leave. Seeing him finally accept my company encouraged me to continue, though this was a story that part of me hoped I wouldn't have the chance to finish.

"After a couple of years, I hadn't changed my mind. Somewhere along the line, she realized I was serious. She knew full well my background and what would be expected of me, but… in what might be seen as cruelty, she supported and encouraged me. When I was twelve, she offered to let me stay late after school to help her with grading papers and putting together lessons. I loved it. My parents normally never agreed to let me do anything I wanted to do, but this time they did. They seemed happy I was doing extra work after school and receiving high praise from my teachers. It gave them something to brag about at parties, and bragging is particularly important for the wealthy. Especially when it comes to their kids."

"Not just the wealthy," he said.

"Perhaps you're right there. I suppose everyone would like to be seen as more than they are or… less," I said, looking at him again.

He looked away in obvious discomfort. "Sorry for interrupting. Continue the story."

"I did this for nearly a year. Shortly before I turned thirteen, Ms. Yates's health took a turn. Her condition only worsened as the weeks went on, until it became clear this was not something she would recover from. She announced that she would not be coming back for the next school year. When my thirteenth birthday came, she gave me a gift: a journal, where she'd made all her notes. She'd planned to write a book one day to help young educators learn the best ways to communicate with young students, but her illness made this impossible. I suppose she thought giving me her notes would be the next best thing. "I mustered up the courage to tell my mother and father what I planned to do once I finished school. I wanted to be a teacher, and now I had the best tool in the world given to me by such a wonderful teacher. Their response was instant. I was forbidden from becoming a teacher. My father had already begun speaking with other families about who I might marry. I was called ungrateful and unruly…"

I hesitated for a moment, not sure I wanted to continue. I'd never told anyone this and wasn't sure why I'd decided to now.

"This must be the good part. Well, now you can't leave. Gotta at least finish the story before you go."

I managed to force a smile, though it must've been a terrible one.

"The fight became quite heated. My brothers joined in, hurling their own insults. My mother was shouting at me. I'd never seen my father so angry. Just when I thought it couldn't get worse, he grabbed the book from my hands. He hurried to our stove, still in a rage. He shoved one of our servants aside and threw it in. I watched it catch fire, and in that moment, I wanted to jump in with it. I always thought, in my naive child's mind, that my parents truly did love me, deep down. They just showed it in their own way, perhaps. That moment I realized my family didn't love me at all. I… my body, and I suppose my womb in particular, was a tool. No different from a hammer to put down shingles on a roof or an umbrella in the rain. A person doesn't love their tool. They just strive to use it in the way that benefits them the most."

"No. I've definitely seen men love their tools. I hated that story, by the way. You ruined that spoiled princess image I had in my mind, and now I'll never forgive you for it."

The deadpan way he said it made me laugh, despite the terrible memory I'd just dredged up.

"Well, if it makes you feel any better, I'm sure there have been plenty of princesses who went through similar experiences."

"Ah, so you do see yourself as a princess. My mistake."

When the candlelight caught his eyes, I felt something shift in me. An uncomfortable and unfamiliar warmth came to my cheeks, and I reached up to touch one of them. I quickly pushed the thought from my mind.

"Maybe there's a terrible story you'd like to share? I'd imagine there's still plenty of time left on your watch."

"Alright…" he said, to my surprise.

Chapter Eleven

Tom Roland

I wasn't sure what compelled me to agree to this. Lying came as naturally to me as breathing. I'd been lying for the last few years, sure, but it didn't start there. Even when I was a kid, I lied for myself, lied for other people, and lied just to see if people would believe me. I guess I got so good at it that it became easier and easier to convince people that what I said was true.

And yet, part of what came with that was having a good eye for the truth. I could smell a lie a mile away. I was good at picking up on even the little ones. But today I realized that the first time I ever saw Tabitha Henry tell a lie was when I asked her to.

I couldn't bring myself to lie to her, so I did something I almost never did.

I took a deep breath, and then I told the truth.

"I don't have many stories about my parents that aren't made up. I talk about my mother sometimes, but the truth is I never met the woman, and she wasn't mentioned a single time by my father. The one time I asked, he beat me so badly he knocked a tooth out. Thankfully, it was a baby tooth," I said, chuckling. I quickly hardened my expression. I'd long realized that I had a bad habit of laughing when I heard something awful, and it was worst when it involved me.

"It isn't funny, you know, but I understand why you laugh. It's alright if you want to laugh, if it makes it easier to tell your story," she said, much to my surprise. It was surprisingly wise coming from a twenty-one-year-old.

"Well, that makes it a lot easier. Thank you. So I stopped asking my father about my mother. I figure either she did something bad to him that he didn't want to talk about, or he did something bad to her that he didn't want to talk about. Probably both. My sister… well, she's made up. I never had a sister, thank God. The only woman I had in my life was a teacher who invited me over to eat with her, and it turned out she didn't know how to keep her hands to herself when alone around young boys. I didn't know any better, so I thought I was lucky. In a strange way, it was the first thing even close to love anyone had ever shown me."

I stopped speaking when I saw Tabitha wiping at her face. A sniff confirmed what I suspected.

"Please do me a favor, Mr. Roland, and continue your story. I don't cry from my ears, so I can still listen."

I laughed, perhaps inappropriately, perhaps not. I didn't exactly know. Though this was possibly the easiest conversation I'd ever had, given the challenging topic. I quickly moved on from the teacher. I'd long since stopped considering myself "lucky" to have known her.

"I didn't leave home voluntarily to find my way in the world. When I was a young man, a little younger than you, my father got into a fight with some outlaws passing through over something so stupid I can't even recall what it was. He was drunk and kept threatening one of their boys. Finally, he made the foolish mistake of moving past threats and reaching for his pistol. Was shot dead before it cleared leather. The leader was so impressed by my lack of emotion at seeing my father gunned down that he asked if I'd like to join them and earn some good money. So… that's what I did."

"Do you have a big fortune stashed away somewhere?" she asked.

"That's the thing about outlaws, Ms. Henry. They lie. Never trust a thing one of them tells you."

"Does that also apply to you?"

"Especially me," I said.

"What happened after you joined up with those outlaws?" she asked. The question I was afraid she'd ask.

"I reckon that's enough story time about myself for today. For obvious reasons, I'd appreciate it if all this stayed between the two of us."

"Sorry you had to meet such an awful teacher, Mr. Roland. A teacher can really affect a child quite a lot… for good and for bad."

I grunted, considering my reply. I appreciated her words, but was already feeling worn out from the conversation and reliving the memories. In the end, I really couldn't think of any reply at all, so I simply changed the subject.

"Why not become a teacher yourself? Does it really matter that much if your family likes it?"

She stared blankly ahead for a moment, as if surprised by the question.

"Yes, of course it matters. My father would personally see to it no one would hire me."

"Not if you travel far enough," I said. "Besides, are you sure he'd try to stop you? Sounds like they sent you here to get you out of their hair. Maybe they've written you off as a lost cause and won't even care anymore."

She laughed at that, shaking her head.

"Oh, how I wish that were the case, but you don't know my father. Or my mother, for that matter. They're used to getting their way, and the world makes it so they are never disappointed. Everything's always more complicated when dealing with rich and powerful people, Mr. Roland."

I tipped my hat, smiling. "Well then, I suppose I should consider myself lucky my life isn't burdened by such… complications."

"Indeed. And I'm surprised by your response. Most men I've spoken to immediately tell me what a fool I am for not happily accepting my place as the wife of some wealthy man and bearing children."

"Well, I'll not call you a fool, but there's certainly nothing wrong with being a proud mother. Not so different from being a teacher either."

She nodded, not nearly as upset by the statement as I'd expected her to be. Had I said this a month ago, she'd probably have bitten my head off. I suppose all you have to do to make a young woman act reasonably is save her life.

"That's well-reasoned. Perhaps if I could choose a husband, that's something I'd consider. A man chosen by my father will be like my father, and that is not a man I wish to marry. Being a teacher always felt like my calling in life. Like it was what God called on me to do. Or at least, that's how it used to feel. Have you ever felt that way about something?"

I scratched my chin. More uncomfortable questions, and as much as I'd warmed up to the girl, I was already growing weary of them.

"Seems to me that God makes a man a certain way, then drops him into the world to make his own way. Besides, I doubt God speaks to men like me. I reckon my life's been touched more by the hand of the devil."

"You'll never be able to forgive yourself until you stop seeing yourself as a wicked man."

"I am a wicked man," I said, a bit colder than I'd meant to.

"You don't act like a wicked man. You've not been wicked to me," she said.

My mind wandered to places I lacked the strength to go right now, and I found my jaw pulling tight. She'd never say such a thing if she knew me. Knew the things I'd done.

"You'd best be heading back in. We'll be changing the watch soon, so I'll be turning in soon myself."

She frowned but made no argument, then excused herself politely. Of course, you give a girl like this an inch, she takes a mile.

I hoped I hadn't made a mistake telling her as much as I did.

Chapter Twelve

Tabitha Henry
Six Weeks Later

More than a month had passed since that awful day in the cornfield, and I was starting to have trouble recognizing myself in the mirror. It was hard to believe that I ever looked down on these people or thought I was above this way of life. I still dreamed of becoming a teacher but was beginning to truly appreciate the life some women chose that I had previously thought demeaning. Raising children, taking care of the home… simple things like cooking all seemed to take on a deeper meaning for me. Cooking, which had once been a novel curiosity, had become a joy.

There was something to be said about the smiles a good meal created. If a man could sit down to delicious food after a long day of hard work, it was as if it made all his stress and worry disappear. Or, at the very least, lightened the load. Good food wasn't just about nutrition and staying alive; it was a means to make people happy. All people.

"You sure you're not lying for Tabitha about these biscuits, Mrs. Henry?" Tom asked.

"Mr. Roland, it would suit you better to give compliments directly."

"I reckon it would literally kill the man to be nice to any woman other than you, Mrs. Henry. He's just trying to stay alive," Terrance said, laughing and nearly losing the food in his mouth.

"Swallow your food before you talk. We might be men, but we ain't animals," Buster said. "You're spitting biscuit on half the table."

"Some of us may as well be animals," Tom said, laughing as he slapped a red-faced Terrance on the back.

"If you boys don't hurry and finish breakfast, I'm going to take it out of your pay," Mr. Henry said.

No one wanted to take a chance on whether he was serious—everyone was eating noticeably faster.

Suddenly, one of the hands burst in, nearly falling as he came through the door.

"Billy's hurt. Fell into a nail sticking out of a fence and ripped his arm open something awful!"

I was the first to stand up and make my way to the door, hurrying out onto the porch where a bleeding Billy sat, holding the bloody shirt he'd removed over his wound.

Billy Whitley was the same man who'd taken me to help with the birthing cow when I first arrived, and he hadn't been particularly kind at the time. I was later told he was quite good with livestock and had done some studying to become a vet, only to give up partway through. He charged much less than the local vet and was good at handling most things.

"Show me," I insisted, urging him to peel back the shirt.

After some hesitation, he pulled back the bloody cloth to reveal a thick flap of skin hanging in a way it ought not to be.

Tom stepped out holding a bottle of whiskey, and Aunt Jane followed closely behind with our little kit for sewing up wounds like these, which weren't especially rare on the ranch. Tom looked far more entertained than concerned.

"Nice little scratch you've got there, Bill," he said. "Must've ticked off one of the barn cats."

I took the bottle from Tom's hand and poured it over the wound, prompting a pained growl from Billy.

"Don't you have work to not be doing, Tom?" Billy snapped.

Tom laughed. "Careful. With him growling and slobbering like that, he might have rabies too."

"For heaven's sake, Tom," Aunt Jane said, herding him off the porch. "Give the man some peace."

"Do you need something to bite down on, Mr. Whitley?" I asked, trying to be as gentle as possible.

"No, ma'am. I'll be fine if you don't tarry."

I nodded, making haste with my needle and thread. Despite his confident statement, he winced and jerked with each piercing of the needle. Not that I could blame him for that, of course. I did my best to ignore his reactions, as he'd asked, and continued the work at a steady pace.

By the time I was halfway done, I'd already started sweating, though at least my hands were still steady.

"This should just about do it," I said.

He looked down at the wound, then back up at me.

"I know I said to hurry, but you can finish the job at least."

"There was a very respected battlefield surgeon who found that leaving wounds open when possible, or at least partway open, led to less risk of infection and subsequent amputation."

"Amputation?" he asked, his voice noticeably higher.

"Right. The thing we don't want to happen. You're a tough one, Mr. Whitley, but tougher men than you have lost their arms and legs," I said, trying to be understanding but also firm. If I wasn't firm, he'd argue. Aunt Jane had told me that the best way to argue with a man was to not give him the opportunity.

"You got a twin sister?" he asked.

"No… why would you ask me that?"

"Well, whoever you are, you ain't the same girl that showed up here a few months ago. That's for sure."

"I'll take that as a compliment, Mr. Whitley," I said, wrapping his wound in clean linens. "Please make sure you go at your earliest convenience and have the doctor take a look at it."

"Why? You already took care of it."

"Because I'm not a doctor."

"I'm not a vet," he said.

"Mr. Whitley…" I said, lowering my voice just the way I'd seen Aunt Jane do it.

"Alright, ma'am, I'll do as you ask. I need to check on a few more of the livestock, and I'll head that way."

I nodded.

Tom waved from a short distance away.

"Hey, Bill. Buster said you could keep that whiskey as a souvenir to commemorate your first big war wound on the ranch."

"That's not exactly the way I worded it, Tom," Buster said, shaking his head. "But, yes. Mr. Henry said you were welcome to take it as compensation. It's a good bottle."

Billy looked down at the label, raising his eyebrows and nodding. "No kidding."

Without another word, he stood up and left. Part of me wondered where my whiskey bottle reward was. Not that I'd want such a thing.

"Nice job, Tabitha. Got our soldier patched up and back in action. Saved the man's life, I reckon."

"I've done more work than you have so far today, Tom," I said, smiling.

"More like this week," Buster corrected. "And you're acting awfully familiar, Tom. Tabitha, huh? Not Miss Henry?"

Tom's face immediately reddened.

"Apologies, Miss Henry," he said, tipping his hat.

"I prefer Tabitha, actually. I'd like it if you keep calling me that."

Tom didn't answer, still red-faced as he and Buster walked away.

Aunt Jane put an arm around my shoulder and gave me a quick hug.

"That was very good work. Let's get you cleaned up," she said, walking with me to the wash basin outside. "We'll have to get you a replacement dress."

"That's alright, Aunt Jane. I have dozens of them at home."

"But you said you liked the ones you wear here more than those you had at home."

That was true. She'd remembered.

"That's very kind of you and Uncle," I said, trying not to become emotional. "I do like them better."

Chapter Thirteen

Tom Roland

I was hauling feed sacks to the barn when I spotted three riders approaching from the north. My hand instinctively moved toward my belt before I realized I didn't have a pistol on me, though I recognized the lead rider before any real alarm set in: Carter Richardson. The old man from the fence dispute months back. His two sons flanked him, and all three had their hands visible and empty, even though they wore guns on their hips.

Still, I kept my distance as they rode up to the front of the house. Mr. Henry emerged from the porch, and I found myself drifting closer to hear what they had to say.

"Afternoon, Mr. Henry," Carter called out, dismounting slowly. His sons followed suit, both looking uncomfortable. "We've not been formally introduced. I'm your new neighbor who moved in a few months back. Hope we're not intruding."

"Not at all, and you must be Mr. Richardson. What brings you by?"

The old man cleared his throat, glancing around until his eyes found me. "Actually, we ought to speak about your man Tom there first, if that's alright."

All eyes turned to me, and I felt my stomach tighten. Nothing good ever came from being singled out by a crowd.

"Tom," Mr. Henry called. "Come on over."

I set down the feed sack I'd been carrying and walked over, trying to read the expressions on the Richardson faces. They didn't look angry or threatening, which was something.

"Mr. Roland," Carter said, extending his hand. "I wanted to thank you properly for how you handled that business with the fence a few months back."

I shook his hand, admittedly a bit confused. "No need for thanks. We sorted it out."

"That's the thing. It could've gone a lot worse if you hadn't kept your head." He gestured to his sons. "Anthony here was ready to start shooting over a few feet of fence line. Might've gotten someone killed over nothing."

Anthony Richardson stepped forward, hat in his hands. "I wanted to apologize, Mr. Roland. For pulling on you like that. Wasn't right, and it sure wasn't smart."

"Water under the bridge," I said, though I could still feel an ache in my leg from time to time.

"We brought you something," Carter said, nodding to his younger son, who produced a burlap sack from his saddlebag. "Best sausage you'll find in three counties. My wife's recipe. Don't get any fresher either."

The smell hit me before I even took the sack. It was rich, smoky, seasoned with herbs I recognized but couldn't name. My mouth watered a bit involuntarily.

"That's very kind of you," I said. "But really, there's no need—"

"Nonsense," Carter interrupted. "This is for everyone here on the ranch. Besides, we're hoping to be better neighbors going forward. Maybe trade some goods from time to time, help each other out during harvest. Nothing worse out here than a bad neighbor."

Mr. Henry stepped up, clearly pleased with this development. "That sounds like a fine arrangement, Mr. Richardson. Why don't you and your boys come inside? My wife just put on fresh coffee."

As the men headed toward the house, Mrs. Henry appeared on the porch, having obviously been listening from inside.

"Tom, that sausage smells wonderful," she said. "You know, I was just thinking we needed something special for lunch today. Didn't you mention once that you used to make some kind of sausage dish when you went hunting?"

I had mentioned that, though the truth was more complicated. The "hunting trips" had been times when our gang holed up in the wilderness, living off whatever we could catch or steal. I'd gotten good at making meals from scraps—sausage, eggs, and whatever vegetables we could forage or liberate from nearby farms.

"I might remember a thing or two," I said, smiling. "Nothing close to what you make regularly."

"Perfect!" Mrs. Henry clapped her hands together. "Tabitha's been wanting to learn more cooking techniques, and a camp lunch has its own charm. Why don't you two work on lunch while the rest of us get acquainted with our neighbors?"

My stomach dropped. The last thing I needed was to be alone in a kitchen with Tabitha, especially after the way she'd been acting lately. Ever since the incident in the cornfield, she'd been… different. Friendlier. More attentive. It was making me nervous.

"I'm sure Miss Henry has other things—" I started, though a familiar voice cut me off.

"Actually, I'd love to learn," Tabitha interrupted, appearing beside her aunt with that bright smile that had been showing up more and more often lately. "I never expected Tom to be hiding recipes in that hard head of his."

Mrs. Henry was already ushering the Richardson men inside, leaving me standing there with the sack of sausage and a young woman who seemed genuinely excited about spending time with me. Exactly what I'd been trying to avoid.

"Well," I said reluctantly, "I suppose we could put something together."

***

Twenty minutes later, I found myself in the Henry kitchen, sleeves rolled up, trying to pretend this was a normal situation. Tabitha stood beside me at the large wooden table, watching intently as I sliced the potatoes and dumped them into the greased skillet.

"You're very good with that knife," she observed.

Maybe a bit too good, and unfortunately, my experience rarely involved kitchen work. "Just takes practice."

I'd already sent her to gather eggs from the henhouse and collect some wild onions from the garden, hoping to be free of her for a bit. However, it barely felt like she was gone a minute. Now she was back, standing closer than was strictly necessary, and I was acutely aware of her presence.

"So what exactly are we making?" she asked.

"Something my… friends and I used to call a campfire scramble. Nothing fancy, but it fills you up." I added the sausage pieces. The sound of sizzling filled the kitchen, along with that rich, smoky aroma.

"Your friends eat things like that often?"

If only she knew. Most of the time dirt would've been an improvement. "We made do with what we had."

As the sausage cooked, I found myself falling into the familiar rhythm of the work. It had been years since I'd cooked anything more complicated than coffee over a campfire. This felt… relaxing. Comfortable in a way that made me deeply uncomfortable.

"Should I crack the eggs now?" Tabitha asked, moving to stand beside me at the stove.

"Not yet. Let the sausage get a good sear first." I stirred the meat and potatoes, trying to ignore how her sleeve brushed against my arm. Didn't she understand the concept of personal space? "Onions next."

She added the diced onions to the pan, and she made a point of leaning far closer than necessary. My face was starting to burn in a way that had nothing to do with cooking.

"Like this?" She stared up at me with those blue eyes and smiled. I had to step back.

"That's fine," I said, my voice rougher than I meant for it to be.

I realized she was still looking at me, but worse, I realized the effect it was having.

"Tom," she said softly, "I wanted to thank you again. For everything you've done for me since I've been here."

"No need," I said quickly, turning back to the stove. "Any other man would've done the same."

"No, they wouldn't have. I've known plenty of other men." Her voice was quiet but certain. "You've been… very kind to me."

There was that word again. Kind. I'd rather be called every foul name that would make a preacher turn away than to be called kind.

"No, ma'am," I said, stirring the sausage and onions more vigorously than necessary. "I've barely been civil."

"That's not true." She moved closer again, and this time I couldn't step far enough away to still be in reach to stir the skillet. "You encouraged me to stand up to my father. You've been patient with my questions. You saved my life, but not just in the obvious way."

"I did what anyone would do."

"You did what a good man would do, if that's what you mean."

I put down the wooden spoon and turned to face her, needing to put an end to this before it went any further.

"Tabitha, you don't know me. You don't know the things I've done, the kind of man I really am. If you did—"

"Then tell me," she interrupted, stepping even closer. "I've told you about my past, my family. You've already told me part of yours. I'm not bothered by it, Tom."

Because if she knew the truth, she'd slap me and storm out of this kitchen. For good reason.

"You're prying too much. Some things are better left alone," I said instead.

"Are they? Or are you just afraid?"

The question hit too close to home, and I felt my temper flare. "Afraid of what?"

"Of letting someone care about you."

It wasn't exactly what I'd expected her to say. The words hung in the air between us like smoke from the skillet. I stared at her, knowing I had to change the subject or risk saying or doing something I'd regret.

"The eggs," I said abruptly, turning back to the stove. "We need to add the eggs now."

She handed me the bowl of beaten eggs. I poured them into the hot pan, watching them begin to set around the edges.

"Tom—"

"Just… let's just finish cooking for now," I said, not looking at her. "I ain't got the patience for all this conversation, and everyone's going to be hungry once the smell of this starts flooding the house."

We worked in silence after that, but I could feel her watching me, could sense her frustration building. She was acting like a brat again. When the dish was finished—golden eggs mixed with browned sausage and potatoes—I started to carry it to the dining room.

"Tom, wait," she said, catching my arm.

I stopped, looking down at her hand on my sleeve. Such a small hand, but it felt like the strength of an ox holding me in place.

"Why are you so determined to push me away?" she asked quietly.

For a moment, I considered telling her more. Enough to make her understand that her attentions were more deserved elsewhere. Anywhere.

But then I heard Mr. Henry's voice from the dining room, calling for lunch, and the spell was broken.

"Because it's better this way," I said, gently pulling my arm free. "You're not going to be a teacher if you let yourself get mixed up with a man. Especially a man like me."

I expected this to snap her back to reality, but the look on her face told me I'd given her more insult than I'd meant.

Chapter Fourteen

Tabitha Henry

I was in the kitchen helping Aunt Jane with lunch when I saw riders approaching through the kitchen window. Three, all dressed in clothing far too nice for ranch work. My stomach dropped when the man in the lead came into view.

My father.

Aunt Jane peeked over my shoulder, offering me a smile I wasn't sure was genuine.

"Go and let your uncle know his brother is here," she said.

After a bit of searching I wished would last longer, I found my uncle in the barn. Considering the look on his face, he might've been the one person less pleased with the visit than I was. We both walked back to the house in complete silence. Not that words were necessary. My uncle had known him longer than I did, after all.

Noticing the two of us approach, my father dismounted his horse. His clothing was nearly immaculate, despite the journey. He didn't know the meaning of modesty. He wore a dark suit that likely cost more than a month's salary for a ranch hand. His hair was styled, even along the edges of his clean hat. He gazed out over the ranch, as if assessing its value.

"Robert," Marcus said, extending his hand. "This is an unexpected surprise. We'd have prepared better if we had known you were coming."

"Marcus," Father said, shaking his hand briefly. "I hope you don't mind. I'd planned to visit a little later, but business took me to the area today. Figured now was as good a time as any to check on my daughter's progress."

His eyes met mine, and I found myself becoming tense as I always did.

"You look better than I expected, Tabitha. Seems you've adjusted quite well to the simple life."

"Thank you," I said. Words I didn't mean.

Aunt Jane walked out onto the porch, wiping her hands on her apron.

"I'm sure you're tired from the ride here, Robert. You and your companions are welcome to come have a seat at the table. I'll put on some fresh coffee."

Father nodded to the two men still on their horses, and they remained where they were without dismounting.

"That's alright. I don't plan to stay for very long. By the time they water our horses I'll nearly be done. I'll just come in and speak to my family. I do hope my daughter hasn't been much trouble for you. I expect she wasn't an easy student."

"Tabitha wasn't any trouble at all," Aunt Jane replied, her voice warm. "She's been a lot of help around here, as a matter of fact. Everyone's grown fond of having her around."

Father snorted, clearly skeptical of Aunt Jane's words. "Well, I'm glad to hear that. I was hoping she'd learn a thing or two from you, you know, her place as a woman. Learning to be a proper wife will serve Tabitha well in her new life."

"New life?" I asked. Despite my best efforts, the words came out quiet and strained.

"Let's talk inside," Uncle Marcus said, motioning for us to follow. He held up a hand to Tom and Buster, who were also about to head inside. "Wait out here for a few minutes, gentlemen. We've got a bit of a family meeting going on."

Tom and Buster both nodded but looked concerned. Father looked Buster up and down like he was a strange horse and seemed to be holding back a laugh.

The four of us went inside and sat at the table. Aunt Jane was away briefly before returning with coffee for everyone. I sat rigid in my chair, like it was the most uncomfortable piece of furniture ever crafted.

Once he felt confident he had everyone's attention, Father began speaking.

"As you all know, Tabitha is twenty-one. And, it goes without saying, a beautiful woman of marriageable age. As her father, I've taken it upon myself to search for a suitable husband for her. Something I thought might take time, given her unruly behavior."

"Robert, look—"

"Let me finish, Marcus. I've been in touch with a prominent businessman named Frederick Bel. He's a man in his forties and has unfortunately had to lay two wives to rest already without a single child between the two. One died in childbirth, along with their son. Mr. Bel is no ordinary businessman. In fact, I wouldn't be surprised if you've heard of him. He owns the largest lumber operation west of the Mississippi."

Suddenly, I felt a chill all the way to my bones. I'd heard Father speak of this man before. He was always frustrated that he couldn't get the man's attention in order to conduct business. Now, he'd found a way to get his attention.

"Father…" I said, so quietly he didn't even hear me.

"Mr. Bel has graciously expressed interest in marrying Tabitha," Father said, his voice swelling with pride. "The union also carries the added benefit of opening our families up to conducting business together. A mine goes through a lot of lumber, as I'm sure you remember, Robert. Of course, a ranch goes through a bit of lumber, and I'd be happy to allow you to benefit from this arrangement as well."

Father looked to everyone. It was clear he'd expected praise, or perhaps some kind of round of applause for his efforts.

I took a deep breath and found my voice.

"Father, you can't be serious."

"Don't be ungrateful, Tabitha. I thought you'd learned something. Of course I'm serious. Do you think I'd come all the way here to make some kind of joke?"

"I don't want to marry Frederick Bel! I've never heard you say a kind word about the man in your life," I said, standing to my feet, sending my chair sliding back a few inches behind me.

"That's too bad. The wedding takes place in six weeks. I suggest you get used to the idea. Now, sit down. You're not a child anymore, and I expect your behavior to reflect that."

"No, I won't sit down. This union doesn't carry the added benefit of anything. It's entirely for your benefit to broker a business arrangement."

"That's enough," he growled, slamming his fist down on the table. "You'll not speak to me that way, and you'll not speak ill of your betrothed."

"I've not agreed to marry him!"

Aunt Jane spoke up, surprising all of us.

"Tabitha should at least have some say in the matter, Robert."

Before Father could reply, Marcus held up his hands.

"Robert, maybe you and I should speak alone for a moment."

"No, I'm fine here. I'll say what I have to say in front of everyone. I don't need either of you lecturing me about my own daughter. Now I see she's somehow gotten even worse. You've clearly just been letting her run wild on this ranch."

Aunt Jane spoke again, despite Marcus's subtle shake of his head. A silent plea for her not to say more.

"We've only encouraged her to start behaving like an adult, just as you asked us to. A woman can think for herself. Surely you and even Mr. Bel would appreciate that."

"Not when 'thinking for herself' interferes with her family duties. Forgive me, Jane, but maybe you're not the best person to advise Tabitha on how to prepare for the role of giving a man children, considering you lack the ability yourself."

Aunt Jane looked genuinely wounded by my father's words. In fact, I'd never seen her look so hurt.

Uncle Marcus planted both hands on the table in front of him and slowly stood to his feet. His face had reddened in an instant, and his hand was trembling as he pointed at his brother.

"What did you just say? Say it again. Say what you just said again."

Father scoffed, clearly not concerned.

"It should be clear to both of us that your wife has lost her senses and has taken on the role of Tabitha's mother in her own mind. Not that I blame her, given her circumstances."

Marcus swallowed hard and seemed to be fighting with everything in him to remain calm.

"Take it back, right now. Apologize to my wife."

"Marcus, I just meant—"

"I don't care what you meant!"

Father's laugh was enough to make Uncle Marcus snap. He lunged across the table. Father tried to slide back out of the way but didn't move in time. Uncle Marcus's fist connected with Father's nose so hard the chair tipped back and he spilled to the floor.

"Marcus!" Aunt Jane shrieked. When her voice didn't reach him, she shouted for anyone who could hear her to help.

"Decades I've listened to your mouth!" Marcus said, already flinging himself over the table and climbing on top of his brother. He slammed his fist into his face several more times. "You don't care about nobody but yourself!"

He drew his fist back again, but Tom and Buster stormed into the house, grabbing him and pulling him off Robert after a brief struggle.

Father pulled himself to his feet, leaning against the wall with blood pouring between his fingers.

"Let go of me!" Marcus growled, dragging Tom and Buster a few feet before they regained control of him. "I ain't done!"

"Get a hold of yourself, Mr. Henry," Buster pleaded.

I looked to Tom's expression and was surprised to see he appeared quite entertained by the whole ordeal.

"You're going to regret this, Marcus," Father said, making his way to the door. "Clearly these cows and horses aren't the only animals here."

"You're no brother of mine. Get off my land and don't ever let me see your face here again!" Marcus shouted, still pulling against the two men holding him back.

"Don't worry, I don't ever plan on coming back. I've always known I couldn't count on you to behave like an actual Henry. Father always knew you were a disappointment just as well as I did. This kind of life is all you're suited for." He turned to me. "Tabitha, don't think this means you get to weasel out of your obligations. The promise has already been made to Mr. Bel, and he will be far more difficult to dissuade than me. I don't suggest treating him as you've treated me."

"Father, please…"

He didn't answer me or even look back as he walked out, dripping blood all over the floor and porch as he did.

After a brief conversation with his men, they all mounted their horses and rode away. Only then did Tom and Buster release my uncle.

He immediately walked over to his wife and embraced her.

"Dear, you—"

"Don't even start, Jane," he said. "I don't care if it's my brother, the sheriff, or the governor himself. Nobody's going to come in my house and disrespect my wife."

She smiled, wiping away a tear on her cheek.

"I was only going to say that perhaps you were wrong for hitting him, but I'm still glad you did. I've always despised that man."

"I'm glad you hit him too," Tom said, unprompted. "Buster and I heard that punch connect all the way out on the porch. Didn't know you were a pugilist, Mr. Henry."

Aunt Jane laughed, then cleared her throat.

"Go on now. Tabitha and I need to clean up this mess before lunch. Don't want the men tracking all this around the house."

Everyone seemed to be in better spirits, except for me. I found it impossible to smile or laugh about anything. I knew my father. And I knew this was far from over.

Chapter Fifteen

Tom Roland

As entertained as I'd been seeing Mr. Henry slug his brother, especially after the way he and Tabitha had described the man, I couldn't shake the feeling that somehow I'd been responsible for it.

After all, it wasn't Mrs. Henry who put those ideas in her head about standing up to her father and doing her own thing. It was me.

I could already smell the consequences coming, and I could see the anxiety building in Tabitha too.

I'd run my mouth when I should've kept to myself. We shared stories, but I didn't know a thing about wealthy families and their dynamics. For all intents and purposes, I was exactly the sort of wild animal Robert Henry probably saw me as. I'd been nothing but trouble my entire life, and I'd brought the same to everyone else. Especially women.

"Bring us another post over here, Tom."

I'll never forget that look in Claudia's eyes. Never. Not in a single waking moment, and not in the nightmares I'd had ever since. Ever since—

"Hey, Tom. You get mud in your ears?" Buster asked. I shook my head, finally coming back to reality.

"Sorry, Buster. What did you say?"

"Why don't we take a little walk?" he said, nodding to the other men to continue their work.

I cursed myself for letting my distress show enough for Buster to notice, though Buster noticed just about everything.

Once we'd gotten out of earshot of the others, he didn't waste time prying.

"Alright, Tom. Let's hear it. What's got you so distracted? I've known you for years, and you've never acted like this before."

"Don't suppose I could keep it to myself?" I asked with a grin, hoping maybe he'd let it go and I could just put more effort into keeping it hidden.

"Out here, a distracted man leads to a dead man if we're not careful. It can stay between me and you, if that's what you want. Though I'm sure Mr. Henry would be glad to help if you're in some kind of trouble. You in trouble, Tom?"

I sighed, shaking my head. Buster's kindness had disarmed me from going to my usual antics.

"That night after Tabitha got attacked in the field, she sat with me on the porch while I was doing my watch. Stupid as I am, I talked to her like she was one of us. I put all kinds of nonsense in her head about standing up to her family and following her own desires. I fear it's because of those things I said that the Henry family had that falling out the other day. And I fear…"

I shook my head, worried I'd already said too much.

"Go on. Let's just get all this out in the open," Buster insisted.

"Well, I fear that this is all going to lead to a much worse outcome for the girl. I'm afraid she's caught feelings for me and thinks we… that there's something there between us. I'm not sure what to do about it."

"And what about you?" he asked.

"What do you mean? What about me?"

"You have those same feelings toward the girl, Tom?"

I tensed, realizing I'd shared far more than I should've and now panicked I'd have no way to take myself away from Buster's attention.

"Look… I'd answer that if it mattered. You know as well as I do that it doesn't. I'm a ranch hand with barely a dollar to my name. I keep cash rolled up in a sock. I don't even have an account with the bank. That girl's a Henry. Her father's Robert Henry, owner of one of the biggest silver mines in the country. He's a household name across most of the country. Besides, if she ever did manage to get her father to leave her alone, she wants to be a teacher. You can't get mixed up with a man if you're looking to be a teacher."

"You overcomplicate things, Tom. I didn't need you to tell me her family history. I know who the girl is and who she's related to. Prefer if you just answer the question I asked."

I couldn't. The truth of it frustrated me. The answer frustrated me, and what was the point of lying?

"It doesn't matter, Buster."

"What's got you so scared of this situation? This is a grown woman we're talking about. She can make whatever decisions she wants, and it's not your fault. Being a slave taught me a lot about the world, if you wouldn't mind an older man imparting a bit of wisdom."

"I'll listen to what you have to say," I said, even though I didn't want to.

"Life's a lot less complicated than we like to believe. We spend all this time worrying about what'll happen because of something we'll do that we forget to do anything. Make a decision and commit to it. You like the girl? Well, tell her and see what comes of it. Think she'll be better off without you? Maybe that's the truth. Make that decision and commit to it. Cut her off and let her know there's not going to be anything between the two of you. I'm not telling you what decision to make, but I'll tell you that Mr. Henry ain't going to be happy if a man flattens his finger with a hammer because Tom Roland's daydreaming about his niece."

"Fine, Buster. It's not like you're wrong. I'll give it some thought. Sorry for letting my head float in the clouds."

Buster placed his giant hand on my shoulder.

"Tom, we like to poke fun at your expense, but Mr. Henry thinks very highly of you, as do I. And you're good at talking to people, which is why Mr. Henry always sends you if someone needs talking to. Sometimes a person who thinks they have nothing has more than they realize, and the people you think have everything are missing everything that matters. Worry more about yourself and don't assume so much about other people."

"I appreciate all that. Don't worry, I'll figure it all out."

Although, I worried that might be the biggest lie of all.

Chapter Sixteen

Tabitha Henry

It'd been four days since my father's visit, and since that day Tom had been avoiding me like a leper. Every time I entered a room where he was alone, he immediately found some kind of convenient reason to excuse himself. When others were present, such as during meals, he'd hardly look at me directly. Even when I spoke to him, his answers were short and dismissive.

The same man who had encouraged me to stand up for myself, shared a deep part of himself with me, and had even saved my life… now seemed to have regressed to the same frustrating, stubborn, hard-headed man he was before. Only now he frustrated me for an entirely different reason.

It was driving me up the wall.

This morning, I'd intentionally gone to gather eggs when I knew he'd be tending to the coop. However, when I arrived, Terrance was there taking care of things instead. Tom's horse, Harper, was in her stall, and the man himself was nowhere to be seen.

"Looking for somebody, Miss Henry?" Terrance asked as he distributed the feed.

"I'm just gathering eggs, Terrance. Thank you."

"Oh, Tom's up on that blasted roof again. Mr. Henry even told him not to worry about a little old leak like that one, but you know Tom. Does whatever he wants. Or doesn't."

I suddenly felt a little embarrassed. Why would he assume I was looking for Tom? Had I become obvious?

"I'm not here looking for Tom," I said.

"No, I don't reckon you are. And why would you be? You two are like a cat and a dog. Just thought you might like to know in case you need him for something later."

I nodded, realizing in that moment that telling me his whereabouts was an entirely normal thing to say.

"Thank you for letting me know."

I finished gathering the eggs quietly, battling my temptation to fling each one into the basket out of irritation. What had gotten into that fool? Was something wrong with me? Despite my flaws, I thought my appearance was at least agreeable to men. Did he prefer a woman with a larger bosom? Maybe he fancied brunettes instead of blondes. Or taller women…

Maybe I was imagining things, and there was never any connection at all. Maybe I'd pushed too hard for him to open up and irritated him, or possibly said something that sounded insensitive when he was being vulnerable? I'd tried to lighten the mood with a bit of teasing. That might've been entirely inappropriate.

It's not like I knew how to talk to men…

After gathering the eggs, I walked back to the house. By the time I arrived in the kitchen, I was lost in my own thoughts. When I put down the basket, an egg rolled off and splatted onto the floor. I clenched my fists at my sides and stomped my foot.

Aunt Jane came up beside me.

"It's alright, dear. Everyone has accidents, and it's not like you to be upset over such a trifle. What's troubling you?"

"Nothing," I said, but immediately knew that was a silly thing to say. Aunt Jane already knew something was bothering me, and I'd done a poor job of hiding it. "Everything. I don't know."

She busied herself with a pie crust she'd already been working on, then beckoned me to stand beside her.

"Talk to me. What's troubling you?"

"Aunt Jane, do you mind if I ask you a hypothetical question?"

She smiled faintly, then nodded. "Of course."

"Let's say there was a woman who had feelings for a man. Romantic feelings. And she thought maybe he felt the same about her once she realized she had these feelings. But then, suddenly, this man starts treating the woman coldly again. Avoiding her, or sometimes outright ignoring her. What might be going through that man's mind?"

"Men put a lot of effort into appearing unaffected by things or denying they feel a certain way. They think it makes them simple, but it often complicates things that needn't be complicated. We women do it too, but men have their own silly reasons."

"What might an example be?" I asked.

"Well… fear, for one. Sometimes when a man starts to realize his feelings, or someone else's, it frightens him. Maybe he's been hurt before and doesn't want to experience it again. Or maybe he feels unworthy."

"Well, that's silly. If you have feelings for someone who clearly also has them for you, why not allow yourself to become closer to that person? Especially when the woman has made her thoughts clear."

"Dear… this is men we're talking about. Don't assume a woman has made herself clear to a man unless she's spoken all the facts aloud and in detail, then insisted he repeat them back to her and confirm his understanding. The same man might know he's about to be robbed on a quiet road because something simply feels off, and five minutes later be entirely ignorant to a woman's obvious advances."

I froze, fidgeting with my fingers. Was that it? Had I just not made myself clear about my feelings, and so my behavior toward him seemed out of place and strange?

"Perhaps this woman should try being more direct if she was entirely confident in her feelings. Though that would take a lot of courage, from both the woman in bringing it up and the man for hearing her and responding honestly. Many men are nearly incapable of being that open with their feelings."

"What if the two were from very different circumstances? Perhaps in a way one of their families would certainly not approve of?"

"Ah. Different how?" she asked.

I swallowed nervously, suddenly embarrassed I was tiptoeing around this sort of word game. Even if it wasn't already obvious, which I was sure of, it would be now.

"Let's say one is privileged and from a wealthy family, while the other has little means. Would that matter?"

Aunt Jane's expression softened. "You mean… with the expectation that the wealthy one's parents would certainly not approve?"

"Yes," I said, nodding.

She paused, laying down her rolling pin and turning to face me.

"Folks often complicate things that don't need to be complicated, but when families are involved, that shows itself in more ways than simple feelings. I suppose it matters whether the hypothetical couple would be willing to go through the gunsmoke and heartache. And just because they're willing, doesn't mean things will end well. It's just that sometimes certain risks are worth taking."

"Can I ask you something less hypothetical, Aunt Jane?"

She nodded, still giving me her full attention.

"How did you and Uncle Marcus meet? Father never talked about the two of you or your history. Were you from similar backgrounds?"

"Goodness, no. Not similar at all. At the time, your uncle was the man everyone expected to inherit his father's mining empire. He was the talk of the town, and everywhere he went, parents were lining up their daughters like wares on a shelf, hoping to make a long-term investment. I was the daughter of a very modest shopkeeper. Let's just say I wasn't supposed to be one of the wares being shown to your uncle."

My face lit up. This had been a story I'd wanted to hear for a while now, and I'd finally found the opportunity to ask. She continued.

"But my father made this kind of apple candy that was my late mother's recipe, and your uncle had a sweet tooth for it. Many days I was behind the counter, and we made short conversation. After a few months of our regular conversations, he asked me to go ride his new horse with him. I thought we were barely just friends, if even that, so I was shocked. I found the question strange and a bit concerning. I turned him down at first. But, the next day, he asked again. I accepted. I assumed nothing would come of it. At first, his family ignored it. One day, he made his intentions clear. It… caused an uproar. I was far from an appropriate choice for such a man. And well, you know where all of that led."

"Do you regret causing him trouble? Or… I shouldn't say it that way."

Aunt Jane reached out and cupped my cheek with her palm, smiling.

"I know what you meant, and no, I don't regret it, and neither does your uncle. Even in the beginning, things were hard, but once everyone realized I wouldn't be able to have a child for Marcus, well… that's when the ultimatums came. And when I realized I'd chosen the finest man to be my husband. He was never upset about what he lost. Of course, he was hurt by how his father and especially his brother had treated him, but I don't think he missed the vast fortune. We get by better than most already, so we are truly blessed. My only regret was that I couldn't give him children, but in time I even learned to forgive myself for that. With his help."

"So this hypothetical woman… let's say she wants the same thing. What advice would you give her?"

"I would tell her to trust herself and search her own heart. I'd tell her to understand that the real world isn't a romance novel, and often a man simply isn't ready. He might behave foolishly. She may have to move on without him and accept that he isn't the one for her. But, dear, no one can know such things. Not the people trying to give you advice, or the girl's parents, and sometimes not even the woman and man themselves."

"If he's not ready… should she wait?"

"Waiting rarely goes well, but it's not as though waiting hasn't been rewarded before. But an indecisive man often remains an indecisive man. A woman would be doing herself a kindness not to force the matter and to decide when she's willing to wait and when she's better off letting things go."

I nodded, stepping forward and giving Aunt Jane a hug. In the months I'd been here, she'd already been more of a mother to me than my own had been in my lifetime.

"Thank you," I said.

She patted me on the head, returning to her work.

Staying in this limbo of emotions wasn't helping anyone. I needed to clear the air with Tom. I needed him to understand my feelings and demand an answer.

Chapter Seventeen

Tom Roland

Tabitha had become increasingly difficult to avoid, and I knew I couldn't do it forever. Every excuse I came up with in my mind fell flat, and I was running out of time and energy to make them. I'd sworn off women entirely for the past five years. In all that time, I hadn't even let my eyes wander.

But this woman… there was something about her. She was a firebrand if I'd ever met one. Normally, women like that were as rough as me, but not Tabitha. She was somehow elegant and feminine at the same time. I found her easier to talk to than any woman I'd ever known. Even Claudia. I didn't deserve her, nor do I deserve Tabitha. Lord help me. I'd never been much for prayer, but I prayed for the strength to do right by this woman by turning her away.

She had a lifetime of luxury waiting for her, and her children would never want for a thing. I'd had a rotten old man without so much as a coin to his name. I highly doubted Frederick Bel would be any worse, and at least he could provide for a family properly. It wasn't like he murdered his wives, so for all anyone knew, he might've been kinder than his reputation suggested. Folks tend to jump to conclusions about that sort of thing. Just because a man was wealthy didn't mean he was a scoundrel. Marcus Henry wasn't a poor man, and he was the best man I'd ever known. Robert Henry chose her husband based on their businesses, not because they were alike.

"I'll take the next watch," Buster said, holding out his hand.

I carefully handed him the rifle and stood from the rocking chair. I simply nodded, too caught up in my thoughts to engage in conversation.

I didn't even raise my head when I entered the bunkhouse. I was just happy Mr. Henry had given me one to myself, so I wouldn't need to engage in any more conversation tonight.

"Mr. Roland," a voice said, startling me. I reached instinctively for my belt, a habit that would never die, and found nothing but empty space.

It was Tabitha.

"Good Lord, woman. You scared the tar out of me."

"Mr. Roland, it's high time we talked."

She patted the bed beside her, and it felt more like I was about to get a scolding from a mother than a conversation with a pretty girl. Mrs. Henry had definitely rubbed off on her.

"I…" Excuses flooded through my mind. All terrible. I took a deep breath and let it out slowly. I'd made my decision. It wasn't right to keep running from the girl. That was no better than leading her on. "Alright, Miss Henry."

I sat on the bed next to her, leaving enough space for two other men to sit between us. She immediately scooted closer, and it took everything in me not to jump to my feet. But I didn't.

"Do you like me, Tom?"

I smiled. "Well, sure, Miss Henry. I like you well enough."

This time, she didn't partake in the humor. Her eyes told me she didn't find any humor in it at all.

"You know exactly what I mean, Tom. Please don't be coy."

I felt my jaw tighten. Lying had always come so easily. I could've lied my way around this bunkhouse with any other woman or man sitting there, keeping my cool the entire time.

But not this woman. Lying to her felt like wading through three feet of mud. I couldn't do it. But I had to do it all the same.

"I'm not sure I follow, ma'am. It seems you've gotten the wrong idea about something."

In a single motion, she scooted right against me and rose from the bed enough to touch her lips to mine. Not gently, either. Not a peck. I felt the fullness of her lips and the warmth of her breath. A surge of panic shot through me, along with something else I hadn't felt in the longest time.

I placed my hands on her shoulders, intent on shoving her to the floor with ease. I had every right to. I had every reason to. I should've.

Her kiss continued, more insistent with every second that passed without me putting a stop to it. I found myself squeezing her shoulders, and without a conscious thought, I pulled rather than pushed. I met her force with my own. I wanted her. Wanted her more than maybe I'd ever wanted anything, and this was more than permission. It was insistence. She was making her desires abundantly clear.

The moment seemed to last forever, though it was probably only a handful of seconds. When our lips parted, I found myself above her on the bed, my hands still on her shoulders. Her cheeks were bright red, and she was just as out of breath as I was. She looked up at me, anxious but unafraid.

"We can keep going, if you want."

She took my hand from her shoulder, bringing it to her cheek. A panic surged through me. A clarity that must've been divine intervention. An answer to my prayer.

I pulled back my hand, breaking free of her with enough force to send me stumbling back onto the floor.

"Get out," I said, quiet enough I wasn't sure she'd hear.

"What? Did I… do something wrong?"

"Get out!" I said, rising to my feet and leaning on the bedpost to compose myself.

Her eyes welled with tears, and she jumped up from the bed, stomping toward the door. She turned to look at me again, and I made the dire mistake of meeting her eyes. They were wet and red, polluting the beautiful, radiant blue. I'd done that. Even her eyes weren't safe from a man like me.

She hesitated a moment, as if giving me time to change my mind, but I was steadfast. I knew what would happen if she stayed, and I had too much respect for the woman to allow it. I tore my eyes away and listened as she opened the door and slammed it behind her.

I sat on the bed again, rubbing my face like I was trying to scrub away ten years of dirt. My pulse was still racing.

The irony of it all was that I realized, in this moment, how I really felt about the woman. I did care for her, despite my denial. Cared for her enough to push her away when I wanted nothing more than to take her up on her offer. Cared enough for her to save her from a man like me. Cared enough to stop her from possibly ruining her own life for a moment of the heart seizing the mind.

All the same… why did I feel so unbelievably awful? Like I'd made the worst mistake, despite knowing I'd done the right thing.

I'd done the right thing to push her away.

Hadn't I?

She'd have a much better life without me.

Wouldn't she?

I fell back on the bed, staring up at the ceiling.

Now she knew I wasn't the kind man she thought I was. A kind man would've stopped her gently and explained his reasoning. He'd have spared her feelings and not let her storm off in tears without understanding.

Maybe this would be enough to turn her attentions elsewhere.

Chapter Eighteen

Tabitha Henry

There hadn't been a single moment of sleep the night before. Each time I closed my eyes, I saw Tom's face clearly. The look of disgust was genuine, though I wasn't sure what I'd done to earn it. I felt sick and humiliated.

I'd been so sure he felt the same as I did, and I thought he confirmed it when he pulled me closer and kissed me back. It didn't make any sense, but somehow I'd been wrong about everything.

Who was I kidding? I guess I really was a girl pretending to be a woman. The best I could do was act.

I went through all the motions of making breakfast with Aunt Jane, but relied entirely on routine. I couldn't put an active thought into anything.

Her concern was clear on her face, and I could tell she wanted to ask me what was wrong. Nothing ever escaped Aunt Jane. But this time, I couldn't answer even if she asked. How could I tell her I'd thrown myself at a man, offered him everything I could as a woman, and made a fool of myself? Perhaps I could tell her another time, but not when the wound was still so fresh.

Tom had not come to breakfast, which filled me with both pain and relief. Uncle Marcus told us that Tom, Buster, and Terrance had gone to fix a section of fence in the new northern pasture. One of the new bulls had knocked it down sometime during the night, and they'd been up since the early hours chasing down livestock that had escaped. They'd be busy until the afternoon.

Just as we'd finished our breakfast, visitors approached. A coach driven by two men, with two other men on horses riding on either side.

"I wonder who that could be," Uncle Marcus said, finishing the last of his coffee, though he and Aunt Jane shared a look that told me they had the same suspicion as I did.

The three of us went outside to meet them as they approached the house. One of the men from the coach stepped down and walked up to Uncle Marcus, smiling and tipping his hat to Aunt Jane and me as well. He was well-dressed, perhaps in his forties.

"You are Mr. Henry, I take it?" he asked, extending his hand.

Uncle Marcus took it reluctantly. "I am."

"I'm Samuel Morrison, and I'm employed by Frederick Bel, as are these other men accompanying me today. I presume you know why I'm here?"

"I think for the sake of clarity, it wouldn't be wise to presume anything."

Mr. Morrison grinned, tilting his head. "Wise words. Forgive me for not leading with that."

As he turned, I saw the glint of the pistol on his hip. Even as a woman who knew pretty much nothing about guns, I could see the quality at a glance. Engraved and polished. His gun belt was well-oiled and pristine. Something about him felt odd. He spoke like a lawyer, but something about him suggested otherwise.

"We're here to collect Miss Tabitha Henry. Mr. Bel wants her to be escorted safely and comfortably to her new home. I can assure you, Mr. Henry, that your niece will be well-protected on her journey." Mr. Morrison's eyes found mine, and it made my blood run cold. "Miss Henry, if you would be so kind as to gather your things."

"You're talking polite, but you're awful rude to be riding onto another man's property and making demands," Marcus said.

"Mr. Henry, I promise our primary goal here isn't to cause trouble for you and your business.

But…" He gestured to the two men on horseback behind him, and both men rested their palms on their pistols.

Uncle Marcus took a step toward the man, and I instinctively knew this would be nothing like what happened with my father.

"Uncle, don't," I whispered, stepping between them. "Mr. Morrison, I apologize that you've wasted a trip all the way here, but you'll have to blame my father for that. He should've informed you that I refused the offer to marry Mr. Bel. Please deliver my apology to Mr. Bel for the misunderstanding."

He regarded me with some seriousness for a moment before a smile slowly crept onto his lips. "On second thought, you don't really need your things. Mr. Bel will be more than happy to replace whatever you've left behind."

I opened my mouth to speak again, but his expression sent a chill through me. In that moment, I realized I was looking at a man who would not accept my refusal. His palm rested on the grip of his pistol, as if daring me to deny him a second time. As if to warn me of the consequences. As if to tell me there's nothing he would not do to force me to leave with them.

"Alright…" I said, defeated. "I can see I have no real choice in the matter."

"Tabitha, you don't have to do this," Aunt Jane said, walking up behind me and placing a hand on my shoulder.

I turned and hugged her as tightly as I could.

"Thank you for everything, Aunt Jane." I let go, then hugged my uncle. "And you too, Uncle Marcus. This is my decision."

Both of them stood silent, visibly upset. Uncle Marcus put his arm around his wife, hugging her close to him. He looked frustrated and helpless. That was also how I felt.

Samuel Morrison offered me his arm. Reluctantly, I accepted it, and he guided me to the coach where he joined me.

As we began to leave, I noticed the two riders stayed behind.

"Aren't they coming too?"

"Don't worry about them, dear," he said. "They're just making sure no one gets any big ideas. Mr. Bel is a man who doesn't like any loose ends. And, when it comes right down to it, what man does?"

"What do you mean by that? They're not going to hurt anyone, are they?"

"And what will you do if I say yes, Miss Henry? Will you gun me down and turn around on your horse to go rescue them? No, as I said to your uncle, our primary goal today was to collect you. However, we are more than capable of dealing with any complications that might arise. After all, one gets attached to people after several months of living with them. They might go and do something stupid. Is there anyone on the ranch who might go and do something stupid on your behalf?"

"No one," I said, though my mind immediately went to Tom. My heart was conflicted. Part of me wanted him to ride after me. To save me. A stronger part wished for his own words to be true. That I'd misunderstood. Gotten the wrong idea. I didn't want him dying for me. I didn't want anyone dying for me.

"Good. Then there'll be no problems."

Chapter Nineteen

Tom Roland

We'd been chasing down cattle all over the property since before dawn. Buster had tried to warn Mr. Henry that corralling them so far away from the others would cause problems, and, like every other time he didn't listen to Buster, there were problems. All of us were tired from being woken up in the early hours after Terrance spotted a runner on watch, but I hadn't slept a wink. Not after what happened with Tabitha the night before. This had been a welcome, temporary distraction, but now it was all flooding back.

"At least we got all of them," Terrance said, wiping a layer of sweat from his forehead. "Wonder what made them bolt in the first place."

"Could've been anything. My bet's on a cougar on account of the little ones in there," Buster said.

I barely registered their conversation at all. I was busy thinking of all the ways I might apologize to Tabitha for treating her so coldly. Even though I thought it best to push her away, there were better ways of breaking that to her than being cruel. But if I apologized too much, she'd see that as me backing down. Women were complicated.

I'd barely looked up from my saddle, but wished I'd been paying more attention. The moment we rounded the corner of the house, two men stepped out with their guns drawn and trained on us. All of us were wearing our pistols, but no one was foolish enough to draw on a drawn gun.

"Afternoon, gentlemen," one of the men said. "You fellas look like you've been working mighty hard."

"What can we do for you?" Buster asked.

"We weren't talking to you, boy," the second man said. "You let *him* talk over you like that?" he asked, looking at Terrance and me.

Without waiting for us to answer, the first man continued.

"You can start by taking off those belts. Nice and slow."

They had us at their mercy. As much as I wanted to pull my pistol, there'd be no way I could win.

And yet, for some reason, Terrance thought that because they were looking at me, he could draw on them. It was foolish. Before he even fully gripped his gun, the first man shot him. He fell off his horse, clutching at his side. Buster dismounted, and I could see in his eyes that he was going to do something stupid too. Terrance's horse bolted. Buster barely made it off his before it ran off too. I jumped from my horse, nearly falling, and grabbed him by the belt. It took everything I had to hold the giant man back. In the struggle, I felt his knife on his belt. Realizing Buster was obscuring their view of me completely, I slipped it from the scabbard and into my waistband as I let go of him.

"Buster, stop! Help Terrance." When Buster finally came to his senses and ran to Terrance's side, I turned to the two men. "For the love of God, please don't hurt anybody else! There's no need for more violence."

The man nodded approvingly, his gun's barrel still smoking. "A pacifist. My favorite kind of man. What's your name, peacemaker?"

"Tom Roland," I said, holding up my hands.

"Well, Tom, you're going to help us out. To make sure nobody else gets hurt, you see. You're going to lead us to the stables so we can make sure nobody else gets any big ideas before Miss

Henry has a chance to make it to town. And lead your horse there too."

I slowly lowered my hand to Hooper's reins, leading her and the men to the barn. Marcus and Jane stood on the porch, watching it all unfold, unable to do anything. I couldn't do anything to reassure them. I had no idea how this was all going to play out.

Both men followed me inside the barn, and I was thankful no one else was in there except for us and the horses.

"How long are you men planning to stay here? My friend needs a doctor."

"As long as it takes. A slow carriage takes a while to get to town. Your friend's fault for thinking he was fast enough to draw on us."

"At least let me ride out and fetch the doctor for him," I pleaded, knowing it would fall on deaf ears. Had it worked, it would've given me the perfect opportunity.

"Not a chance. Mr. Bel doesn't like leaving loose ends, and neither does Mr. Morrison."

Even the way they said it felt like a threat. No good man would employ killers like these. I was a fool. All my false beliefs that I'd learned from my mistakes. That I'd become wiser somehow. I'd been kidding myself.

"Fair enough. I'm just a ranch hand. I don't get paid enough to die for people," I said.

"Smart man. You might just live to see tomorrow with that attitude."

Reading their body language, I realized I'd been reading these men wrong. They were buying time. Not just buying time, but they may very well have been preventing anyone from riding out to get help. I wouldn't be surprised if they didn't kill everyone here just to take care of those "loose ends" he mentioned.

"There's water just out the back there if you boys want some."

I knew they wouldn't take me up on the offer, but I was given an opportunity nonetheless. Both men turned almost completely, alarmed by the idea of a back door they hadn't noticed.

My hand moved to my waistband. I drew the knife in such a hurry I sliced my side, drawing back my arm. Just as the second man began to turn back, I flung the knife into his stomach. He screamed out, dropping his gun and clutching at his wound. He took a step back, tripping over something on the ground and falling.

I'd hoped the first man would be rattled. He was, but not enough. He leveled his gun at me and fired as I charged him, catching me in the left shoulder. I didn't slow down, tackling him to the ground and raining as many blows as I could onto his face. He wouldn't drop his pistol, and the other man was already crawling toward his. I choked, I gouged, anything I could do to make the man drop his gun. He tried to bring it to my head, and I took the chance to grab it and wrestle with him for it. He fired once, missing me completely. After a moment of stalemate, I was able to turn the gun back on him, pull back the hammer, and kill him.

I staggered to my feet, out of breath, my shirt soaked with sweat. I pointed the gun at the man on the ground, still groaning in agony.

"Please. Please, sir. Don't—"

I pulled the trigger, silencing him. A man who wasn't willing to offer mercy didn't deserve to be given any.

I placed my hand on my shoulder. I was bleeding, but not as badly as it could've been. I could barely lift my left arm, but that didn't matter. If I rode hard, I could catch them. I removed the gun belt from the man I just shot, his pistol still unfired, and quickly put it on myself. I mounted Hooper.

"Let's go, girl!" I shouted, and flew out the back at a full gallop. I didn't so much as turn my head to look back. I couldn't afford to.

The minutes felt like hours, or more like days. Mr. Henry's road to the ranch was a long one, before connecting to another that was not often traveled, which then led to town. My best bet was to catch them before they made it to that second road, but as I drew nearer to it, I realized that would be impossible.

Just as I made it onto the next road, a shot rang out. Before I had a chance to react, Hooper collapsed and took me to the ground with her. As she went down, she turned and fell on her side, capturing my leg beneath her. I saw her labored breathing, and I was enraged. The rage masked the pain of my broken leg. I couldn't move, but I could still fight. I drew my pistol and scanned, slowing my brain. What direction did the bullet come from? I saw the entrance wound on Hooper's side and turned my attention to that direction.

Then, I saw it. The glint of polished metal in the leaves. I aimed carefully and fired where I expected a man to be. The grunt of pain told me I'd hit him. Somewhere.

Unfortunately for me, the man I took the gun from had been a cautious one, not having the sense to fill the empty chamber his hammer rested on before a gunfight like a seasoned gunslinger would. I had five rounds. Had. Four now. I fired again. Three.

My vision was getting blurry. The smart thing to do was to slow down, but I didn't have time. He was waiting me out. I'd lose consciousness soon. I watched and waited for a glint of his gun. Just as I was pulling the trigger, a round came my way, throwing dirt into my face and throwing my aim off target. Two rounds left.

I fired again and missed, but struck the tree the man was using for cover, peppering his face with chunks of wood. He groaned in pain again.

I was out of time. I could barely lift my arm and couldn't steady my aim.

I couldn't stand to watch Hooper struggle and suffer any longer. She'd been too good of a horse and too good of a friend to me. I made the decision.

"Sorry, girl…"

I held the barrel of my gun to her head, closed my eyes, and pulled the trigger.

I made one final attempt to pull myself free, but couldn't budge.

I dropped my gun and looked up at the sky.

After a few minutes, and probably a reload, the man approached.

His face was bloody, and one of his eyes was shut tight. His left arm hung trembling at his side, dripping blood from his fingertips.

"Well now, this sure was interesting. You're a lot tougher than any ranch hand I've ever met. What's your name?"

"Doesn't matter," I said.

"You killed the two men I left at the ranch, didn't you?"

"I did," I said, laughing as I choked.

He smiled, raising his gun.

"Under better circumstances, we might've been friends, stranger."

"Might've," I said.

Then the gunshot came, and there was nothing else.

Chapter Twenty

Tabitha Henry

The coach ride into town was mostly silent. Samuel Morrison had us drop him off partway to "take care of business," which I hoped meant relieving himself. He asked us to go on, stressing that nothing justified delaying my arrival.

"Train should be ready to depart shortly after we arrive," the driver said. He was an elderly gentleman who didn't have much to say, either to me or to Samuel Morrison. He seemed almost out of place. "We won't be waiting for the others if they don't arrive before the train departs. They'll take the next train out."

I didn't care if they took the next train out or never made it at all. It only mattered if it somehow meant delaying the trip. I turned around, as if doing so would allow me to see all the way back to the ranch.

Part of me hoped desperately that Tom and the others would stop them. That he'd come riding up to the coach with his gun drawn, forcing it to stop. He'd help me onto his horse, and we'd ride off into the sunset. He'd apologize for how he spoke to me last night, and we'd kiss again, this time without pushing each other away.

The other part of me hoped he was sitting down at the table eating lunch with everyone else, happy to be rid of me. Safe. Ready to move on with his life as if I had never been a part of it.

Either way, no one ever came. We arrived. I waited patiently at the train station while the driver turned in the coach he'd rented and would rejoin me soon. I had the urge to run, but there was no point in succumbing to it. I wouldn't have made it far anyway, and since this was my new life, it wouldn't serve me to anger Mr. Bel.

Time seemed to slow down as I stood alone, looking out over the countryside I'd likely never see again. Thinking of the people I'd likely never see again. I thought back to my first day here when I was just a helpless city girl trying to help with a cow giving birth. How I'd struggled simply not to be in the way.

I thought about what it was like the first time I tried to help Aunt Jane with supper. I didn't know what many things even were, how to mix, how to work the stove, what ingredients made the best stew. How long to bake, how to make biscuits, pie crusts… and the first batch of biscuits I'd made came out as hard as a rock. My aunt told me my uncle and all the men would eat them anyway without a single complaint, and I couldn't believe that. Then, I watched it happen. I wanted to cry because of how kind they'd been.

Then, Tom's face again. The day he'd showed me how to make the hash he'd made in his past… the scent of his hair when we were close. The image of the man who had tried to kidnap me, maybe to ransom me to my uncle, or maybe worse, and then Tom appearing and saving me. If it weren't for him, I wouldn't be the same, if I was even here at all.

Maybe I'd been nothing more than a young, naive, lonely girl desperate for someone to love me and allow me to feel love for them in return.

The sound of horses trotting into town stirred me from my thoughts. I whipped around, my breath catching.

But I didn't recognize the faces of the two riders. One of them saw me looking and tipped his hat politely without slowing. I let go of the breath I'd been holding and finally felt the tears pouring down my cheeks. I knew in that moment which outcome I had truly wanted.

Just as I started to pull myself together, the train's whistle blew in the distance. The same note that had delivered me to the first thing in my life that felt like freedom was now the same note that would take me to my next prison.

The driver joined me on the platform, a surprising look of sympathy on his face.

"This'll be our train, ma'am. I have our tickets already. For what it's worth, I'm sorry," he said, handing me mine.

I couldn't find the words. All I could do was offer a strained smile in return as I accepted it.

As the engine chugged into the station with a hiss of steam and the squeal of brakes, I took one last look behind me at the long road leading to the ranch. I was embarrassed that I'd still held on to hope until this moment.

But the road remained empty, long, and lonely.

After the few passengers departed, I stepped toward the train. It felt surreal. Like my soul was separating from my body and the two wouldn't go on together. My hope instantly melded into pain.

The conductor helped me up the stairs as I boarded, and I found a seat by the window. The old man joined me, sitting across. I gazed out and watched the station, the town, and even the familiar countryside disappear into the distance as we departed. The remainder of my hope disappeared with it mile after mile after mile.

I was going to marry Frederick Bel. I was going to spend the remainder of my life, or his, trying to give him sons, tending his house, and being waited on hand and foot by servants who would never let me experience anything exciting for myself ever again.

Despite all this, I made a promise to myself.

I would survive, and somehow…

Someday…

Things would be better.

Epilogue

???
Two Years Later

The morning sun filtered through the window, lighting up my office and casting shadows across the mahogany desk where I sat reviewing railroad shipping manifests. Never in my life would I have imagined myself in such a place, even as a visitor. Much less a resident. Even my tailored suit felt surreal, as if it were meant for another man.

"Still brooding like an old man, Ed?"

Harold's voice came from the doorway.

"I knew I missed something," I replied. "I finally found where that discrepancy was we discussed a few days ago. I'll deal with it."

Harold laughed. Even though this would save the Oliver business thousands, it seemed he couldn't care less. At six years younger than me, he already had the confidence of a man who owned the world, and perhaps it wasn't all that far from the truth. More importantly, he had none of the arrogance or entitlement I'd come to expect from men like him. And certainly not from men like his father.

"You know, even Father knows how to set aside business once in a while. Growing up, I always thought he was some sort of deranged workaholic, but I'm beginning to see it could've been worse. You don't even look like the same man anymore. I like the new hair, by the way, and the clean-shaved look. Oh, and the glasses. I didn't know you had bad eyesight."

"I don't," I answered. "Let's call it a fashion choice."

"Right. Fashion. You're certainly the fashion-forward gentleman after all. I think you just like showing off that scar," he said, winking as he tossed a folder of paperwork on my desk. "Maybe a little more paperwork for today."

I began sifting through them. Two death certificates. Official. One for a man named Eddie Hall, and another for Tom Roland. Two men I knew all too well. I raised an eyebrow.

"Good riddance," I said.

"Keep reading," Harold said, moving to the liquor cabinet, pouring a glass of whiskey, and sitting across from me, sipping quietly as he watched me in amusement.

My eyes finally found the last page. Legal documents for Edward Oliver.

I choked up for a moment, barely able to speak.

"This isn't necessary, Harold."

"I've seen you as my brother for a while now. I was heading down a dark path in life until I found you walking hand in hand with the grim reaper on that dusty road. I'm a better man today because of you, and you're alive because of me. We don't owe each other anything, Ed, so don't even start with that. This is well-deserved, and Father agrees. In fact, it was his idea. I just went along with it. He said that without you, his idiot son would be out wasting his life with girls in some saloon or dead in a ditch. Now, he has two sons he's proud of, and my advice is you just need to be grateful and let the old man show it however he wants."

After a few minutes of struggling for the right words, I stood and walked around the table, limping without my cane, meeting Harold halfway and pulling him into a tight hug.

"I couldn't ask for a better brother," I said.

"Nor could I, but I never expected you to be this sappy. You don't want to keep looking through the folder? I haven't gotten to the best part. Brace yourself. This gift's from me."

I returned to my desk, daring to hope. Flipping through the pages, I said, "This is a report from our investigator. Tabitha… had a son a few months back."

"Sorry about that part," Harold said.

"No… no, it just means her life is probably easier for the moment."

Harold sighed. "You'd think that, but… well, just keep reading."

I did keep reading. She'd been seen in public with bruises. People had overheard him shouting. It seemed that now that he had a son, he'd become even more paranoid. Those close to the family pitied her for the way she was being treated.

"I don't know. This doesn't feel like much of a gift so far," I said.

"Sheesh, Ed, would you keep reading? There's more in the folder."

"Train tickets?" I asked, holding them up in front of him with a puzzled expression. "Since when do you need tickets to use your own family's railroad?"

"They're symbolic! Here's the good part. I've pulled some strings, and not very hard, mind you.

Frederick Bel has had his eye on an arrangement with our business for a very long time, but Father never liked the man, so the doors have always been closed. He's taking his family and going on an extended stay in Silver City. A few friends of ours were chatting with a few friends of his and… let's just say, wouldn't you know it, you and I were also planning to spend a few months in Silver City."

I slowly placed the tickets on my desk.

"Does your father know about this?"

"You mean our father? Of course he does. He's been willing to turn a blind eye, so long as we figure out a way to deal with this that doesn't implicate the Oliver family or our business."

"Is this really the right thing to do?" I asked, not a question directly to Harold, but more a question spoken aloud to myself.

"When we first shoveled your carcass off that road, it was all I could do to hold you back from crawling there. You're finally fully recovered. I told you, and I'll repeat it: You don't owe us anything. Father gave his conditions, and the rest is up to you."

"You don't have to—"

"Come with you?" Harold asked, cutting me off. "That's my condition. What kind of man would I be if I let my brother do this all by himself? I don't owe you anything either. Besides, you know I'm the better talker, and I'm way, way better with women."

"That's debatable," I said, grinning.

"Give me those papers. I'm tearing those identity papers up," he said, laughing as he reached across the desk toward the pages.

I closed the folder. "Stuck with me now."

"Ready to go and rub elbows with the Bel family and see if we can reach a deal about transporting their lumber? The complete and only reason we're going, of course."

"Of course. The only reason," I agreed.

Please wait just a little longer, Tabitha.

Prequel

Eddie Hall was never afraid to pull the trigger—until the day he had to live with where the bullet landed.

Once the deadliest gun in Garrett Webb's gang, Eddie's life runs on whiskey, regret, and the next job. When a saloon fight introduces him to Claudia—a woman who sees past the outlaw and into the man he can be—he begins to wonder if there's something left worth saving.

Their connection grows in stolen moments and quiet confessions, but one last job stands between them and the life they dream of. When the heist explodes into blood and betrayal, Eddie learns that Claudia's past is bound to his in ways that no man could escape. And when forgiveness comes too late, it's the one thing that changes him forever.

Ride into Gunsmoke & Heartache today, a Western that proves even the coldest hearts can still be broken—and maybe, just maybe, redeemed.

Download the prequel by visiting: claims.prolificworks.com/free/hVHqSBKF

GUNSMOKE & HEARTACHE

Thank you so much for reading the first book in the *Gunsmoke & Heartache* trilogy. I'd really appreciate your help in spreading the word, including telling a friend. Reviews help readers find books! Please leave a review on your favorite book site.

Sign up to receive news on book releases at twistedkeypublishing.com or follow Lila Dawson on Amazon.